Nigerian Wri

GW00385392

Series

***

Agbenugba, Gbenga - *The Lonely Londoner*
Amadiegwu, Justus - *Who Took 'Great' Out Of Britain?*,
   You Are Born To Succeed, Be Proud To Be A Woman.
Ezeani, Geo'Ben - *Redeeming Nigeria Through Massist Ideology,*
   The Freedom Fighters (Drama), Am I Foolish To Be
   A Catholic?, Collegial Consensus Democracy - For Peaceful
   And Better Government.
Giwa-Amu, Anne - *Sade*
Ikeazor, Chukwudum - *The Ethnic Factor,*
   The Report to the People of Nigeria,
   Nigeria 1966 The Turning Point
Iloegbunam, Chuks - *(Panafrica Magazine)*
Omeku, Mike - *Press Structure and Politics in Nigeria 1859-1993*
   A Handbook of Early Cinema in Nigeria - An Introduction To
   Mass Communication, The Power of Faith and
   Positive Thinking.
Opesan, Ola - *Many Rivers To Cross*

Nigerian Writers International
United Kingdom (Zonal) Office
50 Cornford Grove
London, SW12 9JG, UK.

DIED IN EXILE

MURDERED FOR HIS HONESTY

Geo'Ben Ezeani

This book is first published in Great Britain in 1998
by Veritas Lumen Publishers

© 1998 Veritas Lumen Publishers

ISBN 0 9532001 0 8

Artist: Ada Mary Ibeh
Photography: Bob McNab

*Printed and bound
by:*
Orientaliste
Klein Dalenstraat 42
B-3020 Herent, Belgium

**Proceeds from the sales of this book are for the promotion of a
Fruitful Democracy in Nigeria/Africa.**

Died in Exile! Yes, that is the title of the whole story. But the story is about more than death. It is even about much more than going into exile. Why the title then? the reader asked. 'Read and read,' replied the story teller, 'perhaps you might discover why he chose to call his story: ***Died in Exile, Murdered for His Honesty***!

"... the book should not re-open old wounds, but I hold the humble and honest view that unhealed and untreated wounds that remain buried under layers and swathers (sic) of bandages grow septic and gangrenous.

"They will only heal if the proper treatment is applied. In the case of historical wounds, truths, acknowledgement, and an assuaging extension of hands of fellowship are the treatment that will heal them, not official sanctions of silence and avoidance."

"Nigeria 1966 The Turning Point"
- C. Ikeazor

My profound gratitude is due to you:

*Ego Ihenacho, **Anne Gardner**, Audrey Oglethorpe,
Lucia Crewdson, Ada Mary Ibeh **(my little girl-artist)**
RoseMary Richmond, **Sr. Mary Paul English**,
Mary & Alex Bey, **Fr. Martin Asiegbu**, Ann Allen,
Sheila Whitehead,Bob McNab, **Lisa Johnstone**,
Fr. Vincent Onunkwo **and all my** friends and
colleagues in **Tunbridge Wells** and
Dartford, UK.*

CONTENTS

Part 1
In Igbonta - Before They Were Born

CHAPTER ONE

Though Ekemma was desperate to add a male child to her retinue of six female ones, being a new convert to the new White man's religion, she was not as frantic as her husband, Amaechi. "Ekemma, are you listening to me?" the husband called her attention, with a heart weighed down by apparent desolation. "Our people say, 'It is *Chi* who gives a child.' If the mere sacrifice of two yam tubers, a red cockerel and four eggs to *Alusi* Ngene, one of the *Chi* of Igbonta, will result in our giving birth to a male child, who is that Christian God that will not be happy with such a result?" Ekemma was actually interested, but not yet convinced. How could she go against the very first commandment of the new Christian God? *'I am the Lord thy God, thou shalt have no other gods beside me.'* Father McCronny, the Irish missionary priest, had explained to them in the previous Catechism class the seriousness of this commandment and the deadly penalty awaiting anyone who flouted it. That day Father McCronny had come to supervise the class which Peter Arinze, the newly appointed catechist, was taking. Peter Arinze had been received into the new religion two years previously, when

Fr. McCronny arrived at the town to succeed the out-going priest.

Ekemma, like any woman in Igbonta, would be delighted to have a male child of her own. This would accord with the desire and prayer of the people and their ancestors: *Amaefuna*. 'May the ancestral name not be extirpated from the land.' Ekemma was aware of this ultimate desire of every family in Igbonta. But could she help to satisfy this tremendous yearning of Amaechi, her husband?

Actually, it was not the way that Father McCronny, their Irish parish priest, explained the first commandment and the punishment that would befall the offender that made Ekemma a persistent believer in the new religion. Father McCronny was not, after all, a powerful preacher. The previous week, Ekemma had attended the "*All Christians Together*" rally where Rev. Bill Grant, the Methodist pastor, preached to a large crowd in the village Square. Though he preached for more than two hours, Ekemma could retain only, '*What will it profit a man if he gains the whole world and loses his own soul eternally?*'

"Eternally!" she soliloquised. "What will it profit me if I get a male issue in an unchristian way and lose my soul - eternally?" She found herself in a difficult dilemma. "A male child is a temporary thing, but my soul is immortal," she reasoned. She was not going to give in, she whispered resolutely.

"*Nnanyi*," she began, "I have heard what you said. Don't say I am challenging your words. But I find it difficult to go against my religious belief."

In Igbonta, it was 'against the land' for a wife to engage in a debate with her husband or have any open confrontation. Wives usually acted politely towards their husbands even when provoked.

"You know I am a Christian now," she went on, "I expect you would like me to be a good Christian for you gave me your blessing to go ahead and become one. You believe in *Omenala*, the custom and tradition of Igbonta land. And you are a good traditionalist; obeying the rules and regulations of the religion of the land, observing all its rituals. I admire you for living out your belief. Authenticity in a human person is demonstrated when one's belief, words and actions match. Man is good and worthy of respect to the extent that he keeps his word."

There was a saying in Igbonta that 'what a man will do or say is in his heart'. This was evinced by Amaechi's exquisite silence as his wife continued in her marathon monologue. "I will be a bad Christian," she continued, "if I join you to go and offer sacrifice to *Alusi* Ngene." Amaechi looked his wife straight in the eye, and with some air of authority and triumph, he retorted: "I, myself, am not a Christian. But it looks as if I know about your Christ and his teaching better than you. Now, tell me who said: 'Give to Caesar what is Caesar's and to God what is God's'. "Christ," Ekemma replied. "Tell me again," Amaechi went on, "what's wrong with giving to your Christ what is his and to *Alusi* Ngene his own due? Your Christ, I understand, appreciates Mass, Songs and Praises. Ngene, on the other hand, enjoys eating yams, red cockerels, and fresh eggs. If your own Christ tells you what to do - "Give to Caesar what is Caesar's and to God what' is God's" - do you not see you are disobeying that Christ whom you call your teacher and God?"

"*Nna Nkechi*," Ekemma called Amaechi, her husband in a less intimate manner. The name women call their husbands is often dependent on their mood of the moment. Ekemma was no different. Whenever she was happy she would call her husband, *Nnanyi* or *Nkem*. When sad or less well disposed, she would call him *Nna Nkechi*, Nkechi's father, with a tone that betrayed some anger or displeasure. Nkechi was their eldest daughter. Ojiugo was the second daughter. Many suitors had proposed to marry Ojiugo. Some she refused, the others her parents didn't welcome. But uppermost in her mind was Menakaya, a man from Opia.

Ekemma continued, "I'm not strong enough and I've no power to engage in a theological argument with you. *Nkechinyelu,* (what God has given), is the name of your first child from me. You gave her that name. Whatever God gives you, take it - be it male or female, they are equally human beings."

Amaechi was a very good and pleasant person. He loved Ekemma. Though his desire to have a boy of his own was intense, he didn't want it to wreck their marriage. His primary worry was to have a son to inherit the *Obi*. The thought of dying without a male child troubled him. In Igbonta, to have died without male issue was regarded as dying without encumbrance, though one may have had a dozen female children. This was the thought he had not been able to come to terms with.

"It's not my wish to disobey you," she began. "I can't offend my Christian God either. If you want to offer sacrifice to *Alusi* Ngene, you are absolutely free. But you may do well not to betray me, making me a laughing stock to my fellow Christians." She finished the last sentence sobbing, tears streaming down her cheeks.

***

Mazi Chuma Ekwealo, the oldest man in Omaku village in Igbonta, was to preside over the wine-carrying ceremony of the marriage of Ojiugo, the second daughter of Ekemma and Amaechi.

The *Umunna* had finally agreed to permit Ojiugo to marry outside the town. A man from Opia, a neighbouring town had asked her hand in marriage.

It was on an *Eke* market day. Both *Umunna* had come together. Customarily, the presentation of *oji*, kola-nut, to guests was the first ritual to herald the beginning of any ceremony in Igbonta. *Igo-Oji* was the head of tradition, the people would say. Raising the *oji* in his right hand, Mazi Chuma Ekwealo made the supplication:

"Our people, you are not going to die
Igbonta will live
Opia people, you will live also
Let the kite perch
Let the eagle perch
The one who says the other will not perch
Let its wings dislocate

Ise-e-e! the people chorused.

Let the guest not bring bad omen to his host
When going, may he not develop hunch back
What we want are - male issues and female issues

Long life and good health

Is-e-e! the people responded the second time.

He who says I shall not live
Let him go to sleep before the hens
Opia people, as I said, you'll live
Igbonta people will live also

Ise-e-e!, the people gave their consent the third time.

Your journey is a good journey
Our prayer is that good things continue to happen
We don't want bad things or evil men
Igbonta land, you have heard what we are saying
Let the heavens hear also
Let the earth hear

'Offo-o!' the people once again lent their support.

Our land, look at oji
Heaven, take your own kola
Earth, take yours also
Eke, Orie, Afor and Nkwor - Your shares
Our ancestors, you are not forgotten
May everyone take his own portion

Ise-e-e! the assembly concluded.

Okey collected the broken kola-nut from Mazi Chuma Ekwealo. In Igbonta, Okey was a village social messenger. With the influence of the White man's culture, many began to call him 'M.C' (Masters of Ceremonies).

Okey was a lively character. He was as clever as he was humorous. Isiokwe people loved him, especially the women and children. Nobody could resist laughing at his jokes, even the most depressed and saddest in the audience. Even his few enemies admired him for this.

"Mazi Chuma Ekwealo," Okey began, "I salute you. As you have prayed, so be it!" Showing the people the kola, he said merrily: "My people, do you know that this kola is *oji ugo*? What a good omen! Good things have started already to happen." Okey, esteemed by the people for his gaiety, was also very garrulous. He could talk for hours and hours on end. "The kola-nut blessed by Mazi Chuma Ekwealo is a golden kola: *oji ugo*. The name of the woman we are giving out in marriage is Ojiugo. *'Yea-ah*!,' the people roared and clapped.

***

During the next farming season, news reached *Umu-ada* that Ojiugo had given birth to a bouncing baby boy. Being *nwada*, an Igbonta daughter married outside the town, Igbonta *Umu-ada* were to send some representatives to go and see and bless the new child. To make the visit, they were expected to take traditional items given to a nursing mother. These were principally food stuffs: pepper, *uzuza*, salt, dried fish, cray fish, palm oil, tubers of yam and cocoa-yam. *Uzuza* is a mildly hot and strongly flavoured tiny fruit which most women like to use for cooking.

For the society of *Umu-ada*, membership was automatic on marriage. The oldest among them became their leader, better known as 'mother of mothers'. Ogodie was the leader of *Umu-ada* Igbonta, a woman warrior. Women in the town called her *agbala nwanyi*, a terrific and strong woman.

The visit to Ojiugo and her child was scheduled to take place on the following *Uka Orie*, the second Sunday that fell on the *Orie* market day.

Igbonta women were not only good at making very tasty bitter-leaf soup, they also had a reputation for their melodious songs and majestic dances.

The leader of the dancers going to Opia was a young woman popularly known as *Asa*. Asa was so called because of the way she moved her breasts and waist when she danced. Her men admirers said, as she danced, both her breasts and her waist would vibrate rhythmically in a symmetrical unison.

Asa's expertise in dancing could give the wrong signal to visitors to Igbonta. Some actually believed her manner of dancing was an express invitation to lovers. They were disappointed. Asa was morally as self-disciplined as an Italian nun of the eighteenth century. In her, the exotic notion that 'dancing is a vertical expression of a horizontal desire' was proved wrong. For Igbonta women, dancing was an outward expression of an inward joy with the propensity to arouse the same in the spectators.

Asa was also said to have an angelic voice. This must have been the reason some referred to her as *onu ogene*. It was quite obvious that Asa would take the lead in the songs during their visit to Opia.

For her part, Ojiugo had to feed the women when they came. What was needed was already laid down: a medium mortar of *foo-foo*, and of course the requisite accompaniment: bitter-leaf soup. To these were added, a male fowl that had started to crow, plus a fresh gallon of raffia palm wine.

The women, including Ojiugo's mother, Ekemma, had all alighted from the mini-bus that brought them right up to the *ama*, a short but wide footpath leading to Ojiugo's compound. On the back fender of the bus was written: *Drive With Care Life Has No Spare*. One of the women was reading the words inscribed on the side of the bus, *'Eziokwu bu ndu'* (Truth is Life), as the driver reversed to depart. Some were tightening their wrappers. Others were adjusting their gorgeous and flamboyant head gears. It was not long before Asa started the already known song:

"Anyi bialu ineta nwa - Eee nwa nwa
Anyi bialu ineta nwa - Eee nwa amaka

"Anyi bialu ineta nwa - Eee nwa nwa {Others
Anyi bialu ineta nwa - Eee nwa amaka {chorused

Ojiugo kute nwa anyi k'anyi kilie - Nwa, nwa
"Anyi bialu ineta nwa - Eee nwa amaka!

Anyi bialu ineta nwa - Eee nwa nwa {Others
Anyi bialu ineta nwa - Eee nwa amaka {responded

Olisa gozielu anyi nwa - Eee nwa nwa
Anyi bialu ineta nwa - Eee nwa amaka

Anyi bialu ineta nwa - Eee nwa amaka {Response

Anyi bialu ineta nwa - Eee nwa amaka ...

The translation of what the women were singing in Igbonta
dialect is as follows:
"We have come to see and bless the child
O child, O child is good!
We have come to see and bless the child
O child, O child is good!

Ojiugo, bring our child, let's see him/her
O child is a blessing, child is a blessing

Yahweh bless the child for us
We've come to see our child!

Ojiugo's husband, Menakaya, in line with the custom of
Igbonta, went to the *Ama* to welcome the women with a
cockerel in his right hand, raised up. Ojiugo stood at the
uzo-ama, the compound gate, with the child. As the
women reached her, dancing and singing, she handed over
the child to the leader of the *Umu-ada* who took the baby
and lifted him up to the heavens three times, making some
inaudible incantations. With unimaginable precision, and
with some mysterious abruptness, this ritual brought the
song and dance to an end. □

CHAPTER TWO

It was the final day for the preparation of the adult candidates for Christian initiation or Baptism, as it is commonly called. Mazi Chuma Ekwealo was one of the candidates. His wife, Okuefuna, refused to join him. Ego, their youngest daughter, followed her class mates to Church services on Sundays.

The catechist, Mark Dike, following the instructions given by Fr. McCronny, had prepared the candidates for the three stages of Catechism. Mark Dike's previous name had been Odili until the day of his baptism. Fr. Kettle, as he was usually called, gave him the name 'Mark'. After his baptism, he stopped answering to 'Odili'. Mark Dike was later transferred from the Odumodu District to be the new village Church teacher at Igbonta.

Peter Arinze, the former catechist was transferred to a town in the Rivers State, Ogani near Obigbo. Ogani was the home town of Mr. Ekuluo Odili. He was one of the front-line nationalists who fought for Nigerian independence. He later got a second male child whom he named *Nigerianus*, even before Nigeria got its independence from Britain.

Opia Christians always complained about Fr. Kettle's manner of speaking. "He spoke through his nose," they said. "How does the native interpreter understand him?", they wondered.

For the people of Igbonta God was completely a spirit, without any form of body. They also took this belief to be the cardinal teaching of the Christian religion. This explained why the religion appealed to the great number of people of the town. Even some *dibia*, medicine men, and diviners and priests of different village shrines were converted. Mazi Chuma Ekwealo later joined this group.

Many converts got confused the day Fr. Kettle preached his first sermon in Igbo. "Our God is a very loving God," he said, "*onwelu nnukwu ike*"; he has great buttocks, pronouncing *ikè* (buttocks) instead of *iké* (power).

"How can God have buttocks?" the old men and women wondered. This was an abomination for the ears to hear. Unlike Paul's audience in Athens, however, only a very few old men and women got up, wiping their buttocks, as they left the church.

Fr. McCronny and Sr. Isabella, the Spanish nun, were expected that day in the village Church, a gigantic mud house thatched with raffia palm leaves interspersed with holes big enough to get the congregation drenched if it rained. The skies appeared immaculate through the perforations. In some parts, the raffia palm leaves were beginning to rot.

Fr. McCronny and Sr. Isabella turned up late. They arrived when the sun began to set on the Niger.

Both were impressed by the number to be initiated - thirty adult males and fifty adult women. This was their highest number since their mission work in Igbonta, their most wonderful catch being Mazi Chuma Ekwealo. The fishers of men!

The candidates had been advised earlier to consult their antecedents in the Christian faith who would help them choose their Christian names. Some complied. Nneoma was among those who didn't. "I forgot," she lied. Only ten of the men did. The majority said they forgot. Mazi Chuma Ekwealo didn't consult. He didn't forget either. "I'll use '*Chuma*', he said to himself. "I like the name 'Chuma; *Chukwuma*, 'God knows'. And it's true, it is God who knows the honest men and the hypocrites. 'Chuma' is a good name," he nodded, re-assuring himself. *Chuma* is a diminutive of 'Chukwuma'.

Going through the list, Fr. McCronny and Sr. Isabella were pleased with the choice of names made by the candidates. They nodded with admiration, as they saw some specially exotic names chosen by some of the old men and women. Nobody minded how they would pronounce these names. *Marxmilliam, Agartha-Bruno, John-Columbus, Paraclitia, Mark-Anthony, Petronnilla,* etc. etc.

"Those who haven't got baptismal names, come this side," the priest directed. "Join them," Mark Dike, the Church teacher, told Mazi Chuma Ekwealo. "I've got a baptismal name," he protested. "What's your baptismal name?" asked Fr. McCronny. "Chuma," he answered.

"Catechist, what's *Tuma*?" the priest inquired, mispronouncing the name. "It's his native name," he explained. "No, no, no, you can't take it. You've got to take a saint's name."

"What's a saint's name?" demanded Mazi Chuma Ekwealo.

"It is the name of a man or woman who lived a good life here on earth and is now in heaven," the priest explained, with some pride in his knowledge of the Christian religion. "But I like to live a good life, so that other people will take my name for baptism," he courteously countered. Though he was polite, everybody was aghast at Mazi Chuma Ekwealo's audacity. How could one say no to a priest of God, not to talk of engaging him in a debate. Even in his own domain! They marvelled.

With all his education in Philosophy and Theology, Fr. McCronny could not easily explain away why the name *Chuma* was not proper as a baptismal name. The knot got tighter when he realized the theocentric import of the name, *Chuma* - 'God knows everything'.

'God knows everything'. This was part of Christian belief. *Chuma* was the way this belief was expressed in the language of Igbonta. What's unchristian about it? A big dilemma!

Mazi Chuma Ekwealo's logic or contention could not be dismissed with a wave of the hand. This, Fr. McCronny realised soon enough after. He stared at the list again, not knowing what to do or say. He looked at Sr. Isabella. She looked at him. Mark Dike, the Catechist stood still, moping, a copy of the *Penny Catechism* in hand. Some of the candidates were distraught, not knowing what to do. Some others whispered.

It was not always prudent to accept defeat when defeated, though it was a mark of humility to do so. Some administrative experts say it is a grave administrative aberration just to accept being beaten in argument before one's subjects. No doubt, Fr. McCronny was fully aware of this. He had to find a *via-media*. "Catechist," he called, "see me in the office tomorrow with Mazi *Tuma Ekealor*."

"When?" asked the Catechist, "before lunch?" "Yes, before lunch!", confirmed the priest.

Fr. McCronny was humorous. He was a very pleasant reverend gentleman too. But he was not a skilled public speaker. However, the children were very fond of him. They called him *'Oyi umu aka'*, friend of children, whenever he visited or passed by their houses. He always tried to teach them elementary French and additional English. He learnt their own language too and taught them a poem which they never forgot. It's the poem, as he said, he used in his preaching on the Sunday when he celebrated his first Mass in his first parish in Liverpool.

Good Morning, Thank You Lord!

"When the weather is bright and nice
We must say: Good Morning, Thank you Lord!

When it rains and gets us drenched
We must say: Good Morning, Thank you Lord!

When it's damp in the Morning
Very cold to make us mourn
We must say: Good Morning, Thank you Lord!

To all we see in the Morning
Morning that's dull and cold to make us mourn
We must say: Good Morning - How are you?

The children liked this poem very much, though they didn't understand its background of winter. They often recited it, accompanying it with majestic movement of their bodies as they said or sang the last words: *Good morning, Thank you Lord.* The African child loves to sing, in poverty as in plenty.

Fr. McCronny adapted the poem from the second reading of that Sunday. Here Paul told Christians always to be happy and for all things to give thanks to God. Unlike the Irish and Scottish, the English always complained about the weather. Well, they talked much about the weather, especially when there was no issue at hand to talk on.

The Irish, on the contrary, talked much about 'Irish potatoes'. One also heard about the IRA and the Loyalists. Igbonta people, however, admired the Irish priests because of their humane sense of humour.

***

Barely six months after his baptism, it was rumoured that Mazi Chuma Ekwealo had apostatised. Many Christians in Igbonta felt deeply hurt. The Catholics felt betrayed.

Mazi Chuma Ekwealo was a prominent figure in the town. His conversion to Christianity boosted the religion in the area. Many pagans did away with their idols and charms and joined Christianity. His unexpected renunciation of Christianity, therefore, sent a very bad signal. The result was felt immediately. Not many more converts were recruited after the incident. And not many would be converted as Mazi Chuma Ekwealo's apostasy was still fresh in the minds of many people.

'Only fools jump in where angels fear to tread,' the would-be converts would discourage one another. "If Mazi Chuma Ekwealo, one of the wisest elders of Igbonta, rejects the White man's religion, those of us who are less wise would be considered very foolish to accept it," one of the hunters said, as they descended the hill, having missed killing an antelope. "Yes, what an elder sees and shakes his head over, as our people would say, there must be something ominous about it," the other agreed.

The Catholic Church in Igbonta had some active members in a Marian movement called the *Legion of Mary*. In one of their Sunday evening meetings they had decided to send three of their members, a man and two women, to Mazi Chuma Ekwealo.

"I didn't renounce the Catholic Church because I no longer believed in the Catholic doctrines," Mazi Chuma Ekwealo explained to the legionaries who called at his house. "I've discovered the White man's tricks," he said. For him the conversion and baptism of Igbonta people into Christianity was in no way a surrendering of their souls and bodies to any Christ, but to the White man. "They said whatever we have is of the devil. That we have to renounce all and follow Christ. Let me ask you people, Is my name *Chuma* evil? Fr. McCronny said I've to throw it away and take a Christian name. I laughed." The legionaries tried all they could. They did not persuade him to change his mind. Mazi Chuma Ekwealo was a very stubborn man whenever he was convinced of the authenticity of his stance.

Seven days after the legionaries visited Mazi Chuma Ekwealo, in an abortive attempt to re-convert him, he engaged the service of the town crier. On a very early day of *Nkwor*, the great market day of Igbonta, before the first cock crew, the town-crier, Nwugoye, went round the town to announce the cessation of Mazi Chuma Ekwealo from being a Christian and a re-instatement of his native name.

'Titi kom, titi kom, titi kokoko!,' sounded his wooden gong. "May all listen! Mazi Chuma Ekwealo is no longer a Christian. He's no longer to be called Philip. He is to be known and called by his real name, Mazi Chuma Ekwealo. Let the men's ears hear! Let the women's ears hear! This is the wish of Mazi Chuma Ekwealo!

'Titi kom! Titi kom! Titi kokoko!', the gong resounded.

***

The torrential rainfall had just stopped, having poured down violently and mercilessly for more than three hours. Now it was only drizzling like a shower whose outlets suffer partial blockage. The children were still playing in the village arena. Mazi Chuma Ekwealo still had two more palm trees to tap nearby.

The children saw him hurrying, his palm-wine tapping rope strapped across his shoulder. They knew he was late. The night was falling fast and most wine tappers in the village had done their evening round.

Ordinarily, Mazi Chuma Ekwealo cracked jokes as he went to tap his wine, but not on the days he was behindhand, or very late like today. At such times, he rarely responded to greetings from neighbours or passers-by. He would behave like a Board Director who is two hours behind the time for a board meeting, the time of which he himself has fixed. He walked, ran and strode, often moving with awkward alacrity, in an effort to beat the night. But the night didn't bother. It continued to get darker and darker, but not for the children not to see.

"Come, come!" shouted one of the children. "What?" another demanded. "I say, come and see," the first commanded, this time raising his tone. "Come and see," now beckoning, whispering and pointing at Mazi Chuma Ekwealo's buttocks.

"What?" asked another. "Are you blind, don't you see the hole?" rebuked the first. "Yes, I've seen it," said the third, laughing.

"Do you know what made that hole?" asked the first. "No, tell us," several voices demanded. "That hole in his khaki shorts was opened by his constant fouling of the air and regular friction of the lower part of the shorts with his anus," he explained, laughing hilariously uncontrollably, like a bike that has lost its brakes on a very steep road. Some of the children chuckled. The rest yelled, making deafening and cracking noises, others laughing boisterously, except the girls, a few of whom just giggled. Nnedi didn't react.

Some children saw Nnedi as a girl who couldn't say boo to a goose. She often looked too quiet, reticent, timid and shy. Her friend, Ebele, was quite different.

When I, the writer, was young I had a pair of velveteen shorts with a similar hole to that of Mazi Chuma Ekwealo. I was not at all delighted, you can imagine, with this scornful joke being made about Mazi Chuma Ekwealo by the children. Anyway, you know how ill-behaved some boys of this age can be and how cranky in their fun, even about the elders.

Yes, boys could be very naughty and nasty. Fortunately, Mazi Chuma Ekwealo didn't hear the remarks the children were making about him. It was disrespectful and insolent enough to have infuriated him.

Some elders in Igbonta had expressed concern over the behaviour of the teenagers, especially towards the adult folk.

"No more respect, no fear."

Some interpreted it as a sign of the dawn of the new age, 'the era of White man's civilisation'. The village headmaster had explained to some of the elders what this age meant: "the period of emancipation and institutionalisation of unbridled freedom, especially for the young," he said. The people did not welcome this explanation or the new order. The elders in particular were very suspicious of the new civilisation stealthily but gradually taking root in Igbonta.

***

Mazi Chuma Ekwealo was overwhelmed with joy and gratitude when Mark Dike, the Catechist gave him a third-hand pair of trousers. It was one of the three pairs given to the Catechist by Fr. McCronny. He later cut it down for shorts.

Three days before his reception into the Catholic Church, the Catechist made him this gift. For one and half years he had made do with the only pair of shorts he had. They had become thread bare. He wore them daily except on the days they were washed. On these days, he covered his nakedness with a loin-cloth.

For Mazi Chuma Ekwealo the Catechist's gift to him was a big treasure. This surprisingly didn't deter him from relinquishing Christianity when he satisfied himself that it was the White man's religion, used to win the people of Igbonta to the White man and not to Christ.

Since Mazi Chuma Ekwealo had come back from Burma, after World War II, as a war veteran, his horizon had widened greatly. He had seen horror and great atrocities: men mowing one another down as though they were cutting down grass, dragging and dumping shattered human bodies into pits and trenches, as if they were towing bundles of waste paper haphazardly tied. He himself had a close shave with death. Nobody thought he would survive the bullet wound in his lower abdomen.

Nobody was sure if it was an effect of the war but Mazi Chuma Ekwealo was as fearless as he was fierce. Before he left the Catholic Church, he publicly showed his disenchantment with the way Fr. McCronny preached to the congregation. "The Catholic priests," he once said, "instead of preaching, they read to the church people from a piece of paper. If those who are God's messengers do not have the message in their heads, how do they expect us, ordinary people, to retain it in our own small heads?

"Let them look at the Methodist pastors and see how they preach - speaking personally and directly to their people, not with paper. Our people say, 'The blacksmith who doesn't know how to make a metal gong, should look at the kite's tail'," he concluded.

Immediately after the second World War, Mazi Chuma Ekwealo got back to his old profession - wine tapping. People said he was a gifted palm wine tapper. His wine never got to the market. It was always booked in advance because of its uniqueness. Wine dealers talked about him as one who knew all the intricacies of palm trees and every method of tapping. He could classify any wine merely by putting a drop on his tongue. The people said he could also, by the same method, tell which wine was diluted with pure or contaminated stream water. Indeed, in Igbonta, it was said he had no rival in oenology.

CHAPTER THREE

Ego, Mazi Chuma Ekwealo's daughter, was in the class when Fr. McCronny came for school inspection with his team. As he was examining the pupils' exercise books, he was particularly fascinated by Ego's gorgeous handwriting. "Elementary three! that's wonderful handwriting," he commented. "What's your name?" he asked. "Ego," came the reply, embellished with an innocent smiling countenance. "What's '*Eco*,' what does it mean?" the Irish priest enquired. "Ego, not *Eco*," the poor girl corrected with guileless audacity. "But what's '*Eco*'?" still expressing the interest to know. He didn't know she was Mazi Chuma Ekwealo's daughter. If he had known!

Ego like her father, was as convivial as she was fearless. But this time she was getting uneasy at the presence of this man of God standing nose-to-nose with her. The class teacher had to intervene. "*Ego* is the diminutive for '*Nwakego*,' which means 'Child is more precious than money'," she explained. "But what's your Christian name, tell me your Christian name," the priest prodded her. Ego was now all eyes and bemused. "Tell him your Christian name, go on," the teacher urged. "What's a Christian name?" she asked, not hiding her ignorance. "The name your parents gave you at baptism", the teacher explained. "That's 'Ego'," she maintained.

Since she had been baptised and given what the Christian missionaries called a Christian name, Lavanda, by a Spanish nun, Sr. Isabella, nobody had ever called Ego by that name. Only her baptismal card bore it. Her parents didn't even remember she had such a name.

Fr. McCronny explained to the class that they should all be called and known by their Christian names, not by any other names. Any name other than one's Christian name is a pagan name and "Christians should not be called by pagan names," he explained. Though Ego was still a minor, something in her resisted accepting what their parish priest had told them.

At home, she narrated her experience in school to her mother, Okuefuna. "You should obey the priests," her mother insisted. "But, mother, is my name a pagan name? When we were studying types of flowers in school, our teacher said that Lavanda is the name of a flower. Is a flower's name a Christian name?" This discussion was getting too sophisticated for Okuefuna. The only contribution she could make was to listen. Convinced she was making a vital point, her daughter went on. "A friend told me also that the priest's name, 'McCronny' was the name of one *oyibo* food that looks like chicken's long intestines." Okuefuna could no longer control herself. She exploded with laughter. "Why are names of flowers and food *Christian names* while my name is not? You told me my name, '*Nwakego*,' means '*child is more priceless than money*', what's wrong and pagan about it, mother?"

Okuefuna was not a Christian. She had not given the idea of becoming one a thought. If she had had the intention, her husband's conversion would have been a nice opportunity. She believed, however, that good

Christians should always listen to and obey their priests or pastors. She wanted Ego to be a good Christian. She was even enthused to see her express the desire of becoming a religious sister. Okuefuna admired Sr. Isabella, the Spanish nun who gave Ego her Christian name, Lavanda. But not many people believed she would live to see Ego remain a perpetual spinster; no children for herself and no grand-children for Okuefuna. What would *Umu-ada* say of her?

Ego might choose to disagree with their new parish priest, Fr. McCronny, but not with her mother. She adored her. She was also so attached to her mother that the village women, instead of calling her Ego, would always refer to her as *Obinne*, a child at the heart of her mother. Similarly, Ego was so loveable and helpful in the house that her mother also often called her *Obinne*. In her own case, it meant 'the child that knows her mother's mind'. Indeed, she literally knew her mother's mind.

In Ego the two different meanings of *Obinne* fitted perfectly. She was truly a child at the heart of her mother. She in her turn knew her mother's desires. Whenever she returned from school, Ego would go to fetch fire wood and water. She would also go to their farm behind the *Obi* and uproot enough cocoa-yam to make paste for soup. She would grind pepper and add the cooked cocoa-yam to make soup-paste. After all this, she would prepare the bitter-leaf which was by now half dry. *Omnia parata sunt.* All was now ready.

In spite of all this careful preparation, Okuefuna remained the only late cook in the village. Some villagers called the family *oli nni ndeli;* nocturnal eaters.

There was a famous saying in Igbonta among the women folk. This was a recapitulation of the Igbo people's anthropological philosophy of life. "Though several children are born by one mother they are not created by one *Chi*". The people believed that every child had his or her own *Chi*. It was one's *Chi* that determined one's behaviour. Ego was very different from Ejike, her younger brother. This made some villagers suspect that another man must have been responsible for the conception either of Ego or of Ejike. Ejike was so dissimilar from the rest of the six siblings that the favourite argument was that another man must have been responsible for Ejike's conception. "That man must be an *agafu*, a good-for-nothing," one of the three women at the village oil mill remarked. "But Okuefuna is not an *ogba n'ezi*, a promiscuous woman," the second countered. "And even if she is," she continued, "do you think she would go to an *agafu*?" "Who knows?" the third prudently and ambiguously chipped in, like an astute British diplomat cornered by a clever Nigerian journalist.

"Women," whooped Odu Offorma. The three women jumped. They did not know Odu Offorma was hearing all they were saying from his barn. "When will your tongues have a respite? If Ejike is different from Okuefuna's other children, don't you know that one mother may have different children, each with his or her own *Chi*. Same mother, yes, but different *Chi*," he corrected their wayward gossip.

The women might still not be betrayed. Odu Offorma was the husband of one of them. They were certain he would not discuss with any man or woman what he heard 'his wives' say of another man's wife. 'A wine-tapper doesn't say all that he sees from the top of the palm trees.' Moreover, Odu Offorma was a village elder and an *nze.* If other men would talk and gossip like women, elders, more especially *Ndi Nze,* were forbidden by the land and the ancestors to talk, blab and babble like women.

***

Mazi Chuma Ekwealo was pleased that his friend, Ogbukagu, had similarly left the Anglican Church. Owing to their intimate friendship, many villagers had wondered why after all, they had taken to different Christian denominations.

"I have left the Anglican Church," Ogbukagu told Mazi Chuma Ekwealo. What made Ogbukagu take this step was not simply the fact that the Anglican pastor, like his Catholic counterpart, insisted on him dropping his native name in favour of a 'Christian name', but also the discovery that the two Christian Churches - Catholic and Anglican or CMS as they were called at Igbonta - were constantly at each other's throats. If they said they were brothers and sisters in the same Christ, why did they quarrel? he wondered.

For a long time, Ogbukagu, though a local village man, had been following with ardent interest the politics of a government take-over of mission schools in Igbonta. An Anglican neighbour had boasted in his hearing, two months prior to the official take-over, that the Catholic Church would lose all their schools in all the villages of Igbonta. There were five Catholic primary and secondary schools in the town. The Anglicans had only one primary school in the area. This was at Opia, a neighbouring town. This one primary school served for all the Anglicans in the whole district of Kotuka. Igbonta was one of the towns in the district.

Before his conversion to the Anglican Church, Ogbukagu had been a fully fledged titled man. He was an *nze* in the town. Indeed, he held the village *ofo*, the symbol of justice in Igbo land. As a holder of *ofo*, it was a double abomination for him to be present, listen to or take part in any conspiratorial meeting whose outcome would be in any way harmful to another party. Rumour had it that many of the Anglican bishops had not only initiated the move, but had actively supported the government's take-over of all the private schools in Kotuka District, including those of the Christian missionaries. This rumour was peddled most among the Catholics and other non-Anglican faiths. Some village women even said that it had been the main topic in the Plenary Anglican Synod recently concluded.

The argument in favour of the take-over, it was said, hinged on the fact that Catholics had more schools - primary and secondary. In this way, they made more converts and exerted more social and numerical influence in the whole district of Kotuka.

Ogbukagu wasn't convinced with the argument. "The mission schools are doing good works," he said. He enumerated all the blessings the mission schools had brought to the whole district, especially at Igbonta. Sr. Isabella was a Head Teacher in one of the schools.

Though he was not a Catholic convert, Ogbukagu admired the good work of the Irish Missionary Sisters of Charity. The religious sisters of this Congregation had three village health centres in Igbonta alone. The natives were treated *fosa*, free of charge, by the sisters.

Ogbukagu was not unaware of the result of the similar confiscation of mission schools by the government in Odumodu district. "A Standard six can't read or write a letter. Teachers no longer go to school on time. Their girls are becoming wayward. No more discipline! No more teaching! No more learning! Is it the evil they want to bring to Igbonta?" he asked in annoyance.

At Igbonta, pupils in Standard three spoke, read and wrote Igbo and English very well. Some could speak a bit of French and Yoruba which they started in Standard two. At Standard two, most of them wrote and read letters for the elders. There was no town in Odumodu district where children of their age and class could do the same. Many, like Ogbukagu, believed this was the effect of the government take-over of schools in that area. They said that on the day the missionaries were dragged out of the schools in Odumodu district, discipline fled through the window and that lowered the standard of education in that area. "No sensible man," he commented, "would talk about improved standards of education without maintaining a corresponding disciplinary environment."

Earlier, it was rumoured that some Muslims in the neighbouring district had made some efforts to divest the Christians of their schools. Schools were believed to be an effective weapon for Evangelisation in most of the districts. When the gossip about the Anglican Synod first broke out, some people wondered why they who were also Christians would prefer to toe the line with some Muslims from the other districts. Some likened it to the case of the biblical woman who wanted a child that was not hers *divided* into two between her and the other claimant - the real mother. With this measure, none would inherit the child. But in this case, the wise judge made the wise decision.

The thought of what had happened in Odumodu District happening at Kotuka made him ireful. His indignation was aggravated by his rash conclusion that the Anglican bishops of his Church were behind the move. He didn't verify the hearsay, yet he was convinced it was true. "If they want this because Catholics have more schools than us, isn't it covetousness, which they preach to us is a sin? A sin against the ninth commandment," he reasoned. "And this isn't politics. Religion isn't politics," he repeated, this time almost shouting. "If they want to play politics with what others have or with the future of our children, let them join political parties. The Synod of bishops is not a party of politicians." Nobody had seen Ogbukagu so enraged before. His friend Mazi Chuma Ekwealo agreed with him.

Part 2
Life In Lagos

CHAPTER FOUR

Some years after the Aba women's riot in 1939 it became fashionable for families to move to big cities and towns. The Aba women surprised the colonial officers who did not know that Igbo women could be so powerful. That singular incident emancipated many other women. Their horizon widened. Many of them in the villages wanted to travel *abroad* and live in cities and townships such as Enugu, Lagos, Ibadan and Kaduna. Ekemma was one of them.

Amaechi moved to Lagos with his family. There, they were blessed with two male issues and one more female. The boys' names were Adiele and Mbakwe. Mbakwe later came to be known as Tunde, a Yoruba name. Ifeoma was the name of their last baby girl.

Amaechi and Ekemma first named their second male child Mbakwe, an Igbo name; *'if only people would agree'*. At the age of twelve, Tunde, to the bewilderment of his parents and siblings, changed his name, Mbakwe. "I want you people to be calling me Tunde, that's now my name," he told his family. He gave no reason for such a sudden substitution. His parents, brothers and sisters obliged him. None wanted to hurt his feelings. He was a very handsome and brilliant lad. He always took either first or second position in his class.

Man is a forgetful animal. His people would at times forget, and call him 'Mbakwe'. At this, he would either show his anger or just ignore the culprit. They continued oscillating between 'Tunde' and 'Mbakwe' until they all got inured to the former.

Ifeoma, Tunde's youngest sister was a very jovial and teasing girl. She occasionally, though deliberately, would make a joke of Tunde's adopted new name. To goad him, she would call him 'Mbakwe' and add immediately, 'Tunde', as though she only remembered and corrected herself. This sounded like one long name: *Mbakwe-Tunde*. "You are now looking for trouble," he would warn her.

***

It was now dusk, Ifeoma hadn't come back. When at last she came, her mother didn't recognize her. She was utterly bedraggled and looked very untidy, having played all the day in the rain with her play-mates. Instead of scolding her for wasting the whole day throwing mud with other children in the street, Ekemma helped her to get washed and gave her food. Tunde did at times begrudge Ifeoma, his sister, the freedom she enjoyed, and the attention of everybody in the family too. That's the fate and portion of children who were the last *born* in the house - the *Lastina* in the family, Sr. Nkiru called such children. Sr. Nkiru, an Igbo, belonged to the same religious Order as Sr. Isabella.

Being the last born, Ifeoma was the beloved of everybody in the family. Though Tunde had beaten her up at times, he loved her so much. He could not bear to see her cry. "I'm sorry, I'm very sorry. I didn't mean to hurt you," he would plead. "Take this money and go and buy chewing gum," he was seen soothing her one day, after beating her for calling him names.

Tunde attended the Inarende Memorial Primary School in Lagos. Here he met Funmilayo who later became his first true girl friend. Her name, which is Yoruba, means *Give me happiness.*

Funmilayo was a pretty girl, but not as beautifully fascinating as Ovie, a Mid-Western Igbo girl from Asaba. Of her beauty their teacher once remarked, 'No doubt, she would take the first position in any Beauty Contest, she would also take the first position in an Academic Contest, though counting from the back", she added, laughing.

Ovie's magnetic beauty was awe-inspiring. In some parts of *Ani-Igbo* (Igbo nation), people speak of such beauty as *enenebe ejeghi olu;* the beauty that distracts the beholder and makes him forget he ought to go to work. Ovie's beauty was *prima,* but academically she had nothing to write home about. She was an example of how nature could be capricious or even contradict itself. Nature at times bestows one gift with its right hand and takes away another with its left.

***

Not that Tunde had started going after girls at that age. What attracted him to Funmilayo wasn't actually her physical beauty as much as her intellectual excellence. First and second positions in class alternated between Funmilayo and Tunde from class one to five. Like birds of the same feather who flocked together, Tunde and Funmilayo were almost always together. As to be expected, they were envied by their classmates.

Though Lagos was a cosmopolitan and modern city, it was not normal to see men and women in the streets or places of work being together intimately, much less boys and girls. And so, their classmates would always tease them. The climax of this was when Dayo and Nigerianus - the two very funny and naughty boys in the class - composed a ridiculous "wedding song in honour of Tunde and Funmilayo". This, they taught other members of the class.

Nigerianus hailed from **Ogani** near Obigbo in Rivers State. His parents gave him that name in anticipation and commemoration of Nigeria's independence in 1960. They also believed it portrayed integralism and the unity of the country when eventually it got its independence. His father, Mr Ekuluo Odili was one of the great nationalists who fought hard for Nigeria's independence, together with Zik, Awolowo and K.O. Mbadiwe. It was said the North or their representatives didn't want the independence. And so, no prominent figure from that part of the country took part in the struggle.

Both his father's unquestionable spirit of patriotism and his name came to have a very big influence on his life. Nigerianus carried himself as though he were an epitome of Nigeria. He would fight for and even defend Nigeria on issues of little or no relevance. He acted like a hen protecting its newly hatched chicks. In his secondary school days however, he was naughty and stubborn.

That day, all the teachers had gone for the staff meeting. Dayo and Nigerianus had persuaded the class monitor to allow them to sing their song in class. "Now," Dayo began to address the class, "the teachers are having their meeting and we should not use this time to make a noise. Moreover," he continued, "it is about five minutes to the time for school singing practice. We are to learn a new song today from Nigerianus. Everybody has to keep quiet and listen attentively. If you make a noise, the class prefect will write down your names." He beckoned to Nigerianus who came and took the floor.

"This is a special hymn," he introduced. "It is a wedding hymn, and it goes like this:

"Young and new husband and wife, tell us when you are getting married in the Church or Mosque. We are tired of seeing you living together as husband and wife, though you have not wedded in the Church or in the Mosque.

The boy-man's name is e-e-eh ... T. The girl-woman's name is F. Please TF tell us when you are getting married in the Church or in the Mosque. We shall all love to be your guests."

The class roared and bellowed and shouted. Not because of Nigerianus' squawky squeaky voice, for he was one of the worst singers but because they knew whom the song was meant for. It was Tunde and Funmilayo.

As a student, Nigerianus, Dayo's friend was not only very naughty. He was elfish too. One Friday morning, he stood up in the class to ask a question.

"Excuse me teacher! If the earth is round like the English rugby ball you drew on the board, people and things will be falling down from the tip of the earth. How can we be certain that the earth is not flat but round - like the English rugby ball you drew on the board?" "Sit down," shouted the teacher. "Stop asking silly questions in class."

Many of the students saw Nigerianus' reasoning. They believed his logic more than the teacher's explanation. But no one could raise his hand to show their support, not even Dayo, his close friend.

Less than ten minutes later, Nigerianus raised his hand again. This time, the teacher thought he was going to ask a 'wise' question or had something 'sensible' to say. "Miss," he began, feigning to be serious, "*E-e-e, e-e-em*, you said I asked a silly question. Would you please, *e-e-em*, give me a silly answer to that?" Most of the students could no longer contain themselves. They laughed and laughed and laughed. The adjacent class wondered what was happening. And the teacher could not tolerate the insult any longer too.

Nigerianus was punished. He was told to write down one hundred times the last phrase in his question: *'like the English rugby ball you drew on the board'* and was later dragged to the principal's office. The principal cautioned him and asked him to behave himself in class. As he left the office, the principal turned to the teacher. "Don't you think the boy was right? Yes, silly questions require silly answers," he said, laughing.

Nigerianus had been told by his father that if he did well in the final exams he would send him to London University to study medicine or law, depending on his ability. Dayo wasn't happy with the choice his father made for him.

Dayo's father wanted to send him to *Alacoke* University in Hungary to do a course in social sciences. He frowned, thinking his father didn't love him. If he did, why Hungary and not England or America? he queried. In school, there was an on-going story - or jokes - told by students that Hungary was a country of hungry people.

"That's why they are called Hungary," some of the Geography students said.

Dayo's father had decided on Hungary because of its history of remarkable friendliness and hospitality to foreigners. "It was one of the few countries of the White man without a history of belligerence or colonial expedition," he explained to Dayo and his mother.

Not many in the school knew Nigerianus by his real name. He was popularly known by his sobriquet; *Master Tortoise*. He was known to be very clever and cunning. He had a different nick name in their street. Here the children called him *Cockroach*.

Nigerianus was very tiny in physique. But he had the capacity for doing mighty deeds which only big boys could accomplish. Adults refused to accept that he was responsible for the big crimes he committed in the neighbourhood. That was the origin of his street nick name, Cockroach, *'Ochicha melu ihe ebolu oke'*; the cockroach that perpetrated the misdeed for which the mouse is held responsible.

Whatever the negative criticisms levelled against him, Nigerianus was remarkably bright though not as bright as Tunde. He had a puzzling intelligence, though. Teachers at the school were mystified by the level of his logical reasoning. Obviously not *on a par* with his age. As he grew older, however, his objectivity was affected by his undivided love for Nigeria, his country.

When he was in class two, their history teacher gave them a test:

(i) Who discovered the River Niger? In a few lines, say what you know about him.

(ii) Name the first person that discovered America and comment briefly.

He answered as follows:

(i) *"Our forefathers who first settled along the River Niger years and years before Mongo Park was born discovered the River Niger.*

They married and had many children. They cultivated the fertile land around the river and fished there too.

Their descendants after them also lived here for many many years before the first Europeans came. Among the first Europeans that came was a man called Mongo Park. Because our forefathers were good and hospitable, they welcomed these early Europeans and offered them kola nut.

By way of conclusion and reiteration and to answer the question briefly, I repeat once again: It's our first forefathers who discovered the River Niger.

(ii) *The first person or persons who arrived in the land called America went there centuries ago before the parents of Christopher Columbus even met to marry. This was the first person that discovered America. I don't know the name of this person because we haven't been taught that by our teachers. And I'm not sure that our teachers know the name themselves because it's a very very long time ago.*

Many found it hard to understand whether Nigerianus was being elfish or humorous. Asked once, 'How old are you?', he had replied: "I am very old, older than my younger brother. I am also very young, for I am younger than my father." □

CHAPTER FIVE

It has been very long since Tunde and Funmilayo lost contact. Since they had sat for their final external examinations, the West African School Certificate exams, a year and half back, they had not met. Though they occasionally corresponded, they did not see each other all this time. Now what would become of the country in the near future was gradually unfolding. While the North was still boiling, and the East aggressively embittered, the West was getting less confused.

Funmilayo had overheard her father discussing with some other elders what Chief Lowo insisted would be the line of action to be taken by the West - in case of any contingency. She actually eavesdropped on their discussion. What she heard was not pleasant at all.

She also heard them say that Professor Sole was against the proposed action, but at her age, she knew that Chief Lowo was such a powerful figure in the West that even the amalgamation of seven powers of seven powerful professors in the West could not equal his potency. If academic luminaries couldn't change the situation, what could the poor and insignificant Funmilayo do? "At least, there's one thing I can do," she assured herself. "I can save Tunde."

By parental origin, Tunde hailed from the East. But he was born and bred in the West. Here he grew and lived most of his life, except during the war when he moved to the East. His stay there was short as the Igbos didn't know whether he was an Igbo, Hausa or Yoruba. He'd had to escape to Cameroon where he stayed until the end of the war.

In the West he learnt Yoruba. His parents taught him all he knew of Igbo. By association with his Hausa friends, he learnt Hausa. He had a flair for languages. From the way he spoke the Hausa language one would think he had been born in the North.

After class five, he travelled to the North in search of work. He desired to have some experience of that part of the country.

Contrary to his expectation, he didn't find a job in the North, though there were many vacancies. To his amazement, he noticed that expatriates: Pakistanis, Lebanese and so on were preferred to the indigenous job force. *State of Origin* was a major determining factor as to who got what. People said it was the same in some other parts of the country.

Before he travelled to Kano, Tunde adopted a Hausa native name 'Dasukki' as his way of demonstrating his unquestionable belief in the oneness of Nigeria. This did not guarantee him any chance of a job. *Tunde Dasukki Amaechi* his application form bore.

The name '*Dasukki*' passed him off as a Northerner. '*Tunde*' gave him away as a Yoruba. '*Amaechi*' betrayed him as an Igbo.

Because he spoke the three languages sufficiently well, it was difficult to know from which part of the country he came without a personal interview. But he couldn't scale the first hurdle to get to the second stage - Interview! In frustration, he resigned himself to his fate.

"Sadness sadness everywhere, with only few *punctuations* of illusory happiness," he lamented shaking his head. At that tender age, he had started to learn the hard lessons of life - man's inhumanity to man, in response to some accidents of life.

Saddled with disappointment, he began to reflect on the folly of human wisdom. "Why do people concern themselves with the accidents of humanity: language, complexion, height, and refuse to see the substance - the common denominator which runs through all human beings; the humanness of every human person, be they from the North, East, South or West? *Haah*! The foolishness of human wisdom," he sighed.

No one who listened later to the story of his life could fail to be deeply moved. It was a story full of sadness - Rejected in the West. Banished from the North. Suspected in the East.

The Nigerian telegraphic system was still relatively efficient. Funmilayo rushed to the Post Office to send a telegram to Tunde. As mutual suspicion grew and grew, mail and even telegrams were censored by different national intelligence net-works. By mere intuition, Funmilayo had this knowledge. She was cautious about how to word her telegram. The fact that her friend's name was Tunde made it less risky for her in the West. "Never mention his surname, Amaechi," she forewarned herself.

"Good morning, sir," she greeted the post master, a very hefty man. "Can I send a telegram to the Lagos Island?" she inquired. The post master, like a lazy hippopotamus in the Zanzibar River, sluggishly got up from his stool. Reaching out his hand, he picked up a telegraph form. "Put your message here," he bellowed, like a bad employee devoid of civility. *"Tunde, stay home tomorrow. Come assignment - Funmilayo."*

Before 7.30a.m. the following day, Tunde got the telegram. *"Heh*! Telegram! *Otio*!". He wasn't expecting a letter, let alone a telegram. He was very confused and surprised with its contents. But it was a joyful surprise. A pleasant confusion. For one thing, he was sure it came from Funmilayo, his friend. "But why the telegram? What assignment?,". He began to de-code the message. He had by now become so certain that Funmilayo meant she would be coming to their house that same day. The only thing he could not de-code was *'come assignment'*.

At 1.30p.m. on the dot, Funmilayo reached Tunde's. *"Hee*! Tunde, *long time no see. Ba woni*?", Funmilayo greeted, hugging him. *"Da daa,"* Tunde replied.

Unlike the Igbos, the Yorubas were very fond of their language. This remarkable affection made the non-Yorubas admire the language all the more. It sounded sweeter and more melodious, especially when spoken by jet-black and beautiful young Yoruba girls like Funmilayo.

A Nigerian reporter once asked a Yoruba Professor, during the event of the *'All Yoruba Cultural Festival'*, why his people were so proud of their language. "If a people are not proud of their language," he replied, "tell me what they ought to be proud of, that's theirs - their intelligence? Well, the people's genuine intelligence must first of all be conveyed by the people's natural vehicle of linguistic communication," he answered, nodding his head, with some modicum of pride and satisfaction.

Some non-Igbos of Nigeria believed that the Igbos were a proud people. At the same time, what baffled them was that the same Igbos were not sufficiently proud of their own language. "What are the people without their language?," a Yoruba woman once asked her Igbo friend.

At the Ajegunle and Jankara markets in Lagos, Igbo business men and women were sneered at by their non-Igbo friends. "The Igbo language as a language of the Igbos is fast dying out. It's being gradually replaced by *Englishian-Igbo*," one of them joked.

Englishian-Igbo was a form of prostitution of the Igbo language. 'I want to come', for instance, becomes, *'Acholu m to come'*. It's this linguistic adultery that gave birth to the bastard child which many referred to as *Englishian-Igbo*. Some of the Igbo *academicians* saw this development as a genuine fruit of modernity. They were however considered by other Igbo academicians and elders as pseudo-academic.

***

"I was surprised when I got the telegram. I knew it was from you. What I couldn't understand was what you meant by 'come assignment'," Tunde continued. "But before we do the assignment, whatever assignment, *wa jenwu joo*," inviting Funmilayo for a meal.

He was about to have his lunch when Funmilayo arrived. He had prepared for himself a half cigarette cup of *garri*. Tunde wasn't a big eater. Funmilayo wasn't either. Her attitude to or appetite for food was acquired, not natural. Nigerian girls, especially those in big cities like Lagos, were very finicky about their weight. Most of them wanted to maintain what they called a *figure* 8.

By keeping a slim shape, many thought they would attract suitors easily. It had become so trendy in Lagos that most Lagos girls forgot there were men who specifically preferred plumpish women. They were proud to have *'thick madams'* as their wives. It was a matter of choice.

Tunde didn't know how hungry Funmilayo was. It was not polite to ask one's guests how hungry they were. Customarily, sufficient food was prepared for the visitor. It was better to have one's visitor have more than less.

Tunde briskly prepared an additional *iba*, as it's called by the Yorubas. It was one and a half cigarette cups. Before Funmilayo knew and offered to come and help, he was out from the kitchen with a plate of *garri* - oozing out smoke like British train passengers emitting steam from their mouths during the winter in a London railway station.

With Tunde, Funmilayo felt very much at home. She didn't need to pretend to look good or polite.

For years she could not remember when she had ever finished a cup of *garri,* not in recent years when she, like other young girls, became very conscious of her weight and shape. Today was different.

Quietly, gracefully and meticulously, she went on swallowing her *foo-foo*, rolled in very tiny lumps, the size an African baby of twelve months is initiated on. The African mother starts with a very tiny piece to train her baby to eat *foo-foo*. Seeing her eat, one would imagine no action was taking place.

Intermittently, she raised her head, dimming her eyes. Dimpling her cheeks, she eyed Tunde. Bending down again, she made a graceful and innocent smile. Her eyes were as beautiful as they were electrifying. So charming and enticing were those eyes that one could mistake her for a seducer. But that was not Funmilayo. It was just her nature. Part of the beautiful characteristics nature bestowed on her.

Before Tunde finished his own portion, Funmilayo's had vanished. "You must be very hungry, *Fumi*," Tunde teased her. Humorously, she replied, "Not only very hungry, *joo*, but the soup was very tasty. And so, the temptation is irresistible."

Some Igbo women were famed for their bitter-leaf soup. Funmilayo had not eaten *foo-foo* with bitter-leaf soup before that visit. If she had, not one made by an Igbonta woman such as Ekemma, Tunde's mother.

Among all Igbo women, there's something unique about bitter-leaf soup cooked by Igbonta women. Traders travelling to, or coming back from Lagos always made stop-overs at Umunede or Ore to eat *foo-foo* at different 'Igbonta Special' restaurants. It would be difficult to find a single trader from Aba, Umuahia, Onitsha, Benin, Ibadan or Lagos who didn't know what *'Igbonta Special'* meant; special bitter-leaf soup made by an Igbonta woman.

Ogudo, a boy of twelve, and a new apprentice to a business tycoon in Onitsha Main Market, was said to have spent a large part of the capital given to him by his master. This was intended for purchasing motor spare parts in Lagos. On Ogudo's first journey to Lagos, their bus stopped at Umunede for lunch. After spending N20.00, his meal money, he asked 'Madam' for an additional plate of bitter-leaf soup costing N50.00. "You mean without *foo-foo*?," Madam wanted to make sure. "Yes, without *foo-foo*, only soup," the boy concurred.

***

Not until after they had exchanged the necessary pleasantries - remembering their childhood days - did she begin to introduce the pre-eminent purpose of her visit.

"You may have wondered why you hadn't heard from me for so long," she began. "I also wondered why I hadn't heard from you either," she added, giggling, as girls in a lighter mood always do.

"Tunde, what do you think of the present situation in the country?" she asked, still composed but with a very piercing look. He did not respond, seeming rather bemused and stupefied. "I mean, the spiralling turmoil," she added, by way of clarification. "Well, I don't know where this country is heading," he managed to say. "I'll be travelling to Ibadan very early tomorrow morning," she said, breaking the coherency of the discussion. "Today is the only day I could spare to come and see you. The matter is so vital that some personal sacrifice is necessary. Yorubas have a saying, your people have it too, I suppose, 'When a man finds a precious treasure, he doesn't hesitate to sell his barn.' In brief, I've a moral responsibility towards you. That's why I've come."

She had given some hint. The message, however, was not yet clear. Pondering on what she had already said, Tunde was still full of expectation and on the *qui vive* to hear more of what she had to say. She had not come to the point. This, he was sure of.

"I'm aware you know I haven't made my point. My message to you is short. It's also simple. I don't think it's safe for you people to continue to stay in Lagos. Don't ask me what I mean. Don't ask me how I know. I know men like to ask this type of question." Tunde had actually wanted to ask these questions but for her pre-emptive 'don'ts'. And so she continued, "The present *wahala* in the country, nobody knows when it will end. And when the real *kata-kata* begins, I'm sure, there'll be no place to hide, *e-e-m* ... even in Lagos." "No place to hide!" Tunde repeated to himself. "No place to hide," the phrase kept ringing in his head.

There was turmoil in the North and southerners were being massacred there; with pandemonium in the West there was nowhere for Tunde to hide in Lagos, and nowhere to hide even in Biafra, his own homeland. Biafra had become an independent republic and his true identity as an Igbo or an easterner was doubted there. He had to escape to the neighbouring country, Cameroon during the war. No sooner than the war ended than Tunde travelled back to Lagos. He felt more at home in Lagos than anywhere else. □

Part Three
After The Nigerian-Biafran War

CHAPTER SIX

For the past seven market days, Igbonta, both *Home* and *Abroad* had been mourning the death of their traditional ruler, Eze Onyekineso. Since the people of Igbonta have abolished the traditional system of kingship by inheritance, many eyes were on Amaechi as the most likely person for the candidacy. The rumour had even spread, not only in Igbonta, but also to the neighbouring towns and villages that Amaechi would be the next king of the town. Amaechi was well known both within and outside Igbonta. He was loved by children for his jokes and remarkable sense of humour. Moreover, he was very charitable. Young men and women of the town respected him for his uprightness and his uncompromising stance on truth. Neighbouring towns knew him as an apostle of justice. He never hesitated or compromised if justice required that he or his people should be the losers. As an *Nze,* an *ozo*-titled man, he believed vehemently in the strict observance of the laws and regulations of *nze*, as handed down by the ancestors. Many knew him as one of the few prominent figures of Igbonta who were not corrupted by modern civilisation.

Amaechi's uncompromising stand on issues of justice and truth, though it endeared him to many young men and women of the town and beyond, was also a very big thorn in his flesh. He was hated by some of his fellow elders of Igbonta on account of this. "He wants to show us he is the only wise and good person in the town," Nze Olikagu remarked. They were coming back from the village meeting.

Amaechi had insisted at the meeting of the village elders that the piece of land in dispute belonged to the widow, Enyinna, whose husband had died during the last farming season. He arrived home that night tired.

It was about 1.30a.m. when Amaechi woke up. The time of night known as *ndeli* in Igbonta. Night had engulfed the entire earth. Nature was fast asleep. Complete calm, peace and silence had descended on the whole universe. As though it didn't prize quietude, one nocturnal black and white bird with horrific red eyes made a weird cry; the voice very much subdued, but still very audible. The sound was uncanny enough to suggest it was not a terrestrial bird. (I don't think it was celestial either.) It must have come from an unknown spirit world.

Such birds or their visits were not common in Igbonta. That was why their sudden appearance aroused fear and anxiety. They belonged to the category of birds recognised as harbingers of imminent and eminent evil omen. *Ndeli* was also the time when the spirits of the wicked hovered round and round the town looking for innocent and unsuspecting victims whose souls they would pluck away.

This was the time when Amaechi woke up. He sat on the bed for more than ten minutes, wondering whether to wake his wife and narrate the episode to her. He looked at the wall-clock illumined by the diamond dots. 1.45a.m.

It was still *ndeli*. The *via-media* between midnight and deep-night.

"Yes, I've to wake her up," he muttered to himself, "Our people say that the toad doesn't run at noon in vain. Neither does a cocoa-yam stem make a cracking sound without being disturbed by an external stimulus. I ought to wake her." Tip-toeing, he entered his wife's sleeping room.

Ekemma was sleeping in the next room adjacent to her husband's. Ifeoma, their last child was sleeping in the same room with her. How could he talk with Ekemma without awakening Ifeoma? Children of her age had the sixth sense which informed them there must be something very grave or ominous when one's parents or elders were seen in discussion during the most sacred period of the night, *ndeli*.

He overcame his dilemma when he remembered that Ifeoma was a good sleeper. Once asleep nothing would wake her till the following morning. Not even the native mortar gun sounds whose echo would resound in the neighbouring towns and villages of Igbonta would rouse her. Unlike her brothers and sisters Ifeoma would never get up in the night to go and answer the call of nature - even the short one.

"I hope it's all right," Ekemma enquired, still feeling sleepy and drowsy. "Yes, there's no trouble," Amaechi assured her. "Get up, I've something to tell you." "Must it be at this time of the night? Did you not look at the clock, do you know what the clock says now?" "I do," her husband answered.

"*Ee-ee ee-ee*," he cleared his throat. "Ekemma, are you listening?" 'Yes,' she nodded, still surprised. "Our people say, 'To see certain things and keep silent is an abomination that dooms the elder. But to speak and not to be listened to by the youth brings them ill luck.' That's why I took a firm decision to speak out to you this night.

"You may wonder how grievous the matter is that it must be discussed at this time of the night - when both human beings and good spirits are having their rest, when only the spirits of the malevolent are hovering around looking for mischievous things to do. Don't get worried.

"You have not offended me, neither have you sinned against the land of Igbonta. You have not aborted a child in your womb which is the highest taboo against the land. It's also the greatest *nso* against *Chi* and mankind - the deliberate and callous taking away of an innocent and defenceless life." Ekemma was inwardly getting restless. She didn't know if this was the main topic or just an exordium to the subject. She maintained her dignified composure like a disciplined soldier who hasn't taken part in a *coup d'état*. She continued to listen very attentively until she realized that if she didn't come in her husband would go on perambulating around the same topic. "Why all this talk about abortion and abomination in the land?" she queried.

"I'm coming," Amaechi continued. "As I said earlier, you haven't offended me or the land. You have not followed another woman's husband. You have not disgraced our family name; you haven't harvested another woman's cassava. Our children are doing well. We are very proud of them. Ifeoma is taking after you. She'll make a good wife and a good mother.

"I'm sorry I woke you up at this time of the night. The elders say this is the most sacred of the hours of the night when an elder should discuss issues of grave importance with his wife, eldest son or with a fellow elder. This is the hour that keeps away all human distraction. It is the hour when the human ears hear only one voice speaking to their human heart and head. It's the hour of the night when the spirits of our ancestors choose to speak to their people through the voice of the elders - the living ancestors. I've a very important matter to discuss with you."

Ekemma was now getting irritated but still very inquisitive and eager to hear the main issue. As a disciplined woman, she hid her irritation.

"I dreamt a dream," Amaechi landed at last. "Four market days ago, my grandfather appeared to me in a dream. I was delighted to see him. I asked him about my father, my mother and Okezie, my elder brother. Surprisingly, he wasn't ready for such filial and expected enquiries. Why shouldn't he tell me about our deceased kinsmen and women amongst whom he dwells in the land of the ancestors? Does it mean he had no time for such exchange of pleasantries? I asked myself. Instead, he looked me straight in the eyes and asked: 'What's your name?' The intimacy immediately disappeared. You can imagine how I felt. I became very much afraid. In fear and trembling I replied reluctantly, but irresistibly: *'Amaechi, Onyemaechi'*. He went on: 'Do you know what that name means?' 'What?' he asked again. Timidly, I explained: 'Who knows tomorrow?' "Well done," he said, this time his face beaming with a smile. "Do you know tomorrow?" he queried again. I said, 'No, grandpa'. Then, he cautioned, "If you don't know tomorrow, know at least that 'tomorrow is always pregnant and nobody knows what it's going to give birth to. Remember that it's the fire wood one fetched during the dry season that one uses in the rainy period. A word of wisdom is enough for the wise. I've given you two." With these last words, he vanished. For the past four market days, I've been ruminating over this dream. What do you make of it, Ekemma?"

***

Amaechi, Tunde's father, didn't make any fuss about Tunde's choice of Lagos as a place to live or about his preferring other people to his own people, if one may put it that way. Tunde knew and spoke Hausa, Igbo and Yoruba. He always preferred speaking Yoruba to using any other of the major Nigerian languages. When spoken to by his parents in Igbo, he often replied in Yoruba, though he tried to speak in Hausa whenever he was with his Hausa friends. With others, he would speak the Lagos version of English known as *pigeon English*. You may be wondering how it is spoken. It is better listened to than described.

Nobody in Amaechi's family complained. "It is a matter of personal choice," they would say. "What matters is not the type of language or expression one uses," his mother once told a neighbour. "It would only matter if the other did not know the language."

Tunde was so *westernised* that he knew little or nothing about the East. Amaechi got increasingly worried as he became older. It's all about Tunde, "my brilliant son". "What will become of him tomorrow if he doesn't know about his homestead today?" he asked himself. "'He who doesn't know his root is a vagabond,' our people say. Is Tunde, Mbakwe my child, child of my own seed going to be a vagabond? God forbid! My father begot me. After my birth, he looked at the heavens, he looked at the earth. He searched and searched. He thought man's thought. Of all the names in our land, he gave me AMAECHI, *'Who knows tomorrow?'"* Still speaking to himself, "Who asks, 'What's in a name?' There is much in a name. At least I know that my name is pregnant with meaning - Amaechi, Amaechi, Amaechi," he muttered, as one coming to full consciousness after a lengthy phase of trance.

Amaechi still remembered his grandfather's last words to him. His grandfather had died when he was a teenage apprentice in Lagos. He had gone home that year during the Christmas period.

'My child,' his grandfather began, after welcoming him back again, 'your bathing still revolves round your belly. But I don't blame you. You are still an infant. You will gain knowledge when you reach maturity. To be knowledgeable, you must be closer to the elders. You must also listen to them.

'The elders pass on their message mainly by the use of proverbs. To discover and learn the wisdom of your forefathers, to be able to enter into the immensity of the knowledge and philosophy of the elders, you must dig the grave of their proverbs.

'A free-born son of the land who knows not the proverbs of the people is an *ofeke,* a useless person.'

Amaechi's grandfather wasn't a man of many words. Before he travelled to join his ancestors, his words, be it private advice, or public speeches made in the village arena, were always brief and short, often taking the form of proverbs. So was the advice he gave to his grandson, Amaechi, believing he would soon come to understand the manner the elders spoke.

He said in conclusion,

"Now, take this message, my son.
Always try to be honest in life.
Never covet another's property.
Don't be a liar either.
Our people say: Truth is life. Be wise. Never be lazy.
Don't be an ofeke, *a worthless fellow.*

You should never insult your elders, my child.
You should always respect them.
The elders are your fathers.
The child who lifts up his father,
will have his eyes blind-folded
by his father's loincloth.
Finally, he to whom the mantle of kingship is due
must first learn to be a servant to the king.
He who's going to be an ambusher,
must first learn to be a good friend of patience.

Are you listening my son?...

He nodded. *'You can now go and get me my snuff-box,'* the
old man concluded, his right hand now jerking turbulently.

After his reverie, Amaechi concluded that he would
map out an *Ana-obi* for Tunde, his son. "That will bring
him home often," he assured himself. In Igbonta it was a
customary obligation for one to build one's permanent
home of residence in one's *Ana-obi*. The house so built
was to be inherited from generation to generation by the
eldest male child of the father. And so Tunde's *Ana-obi*,
with all the palm trees, cocoa-nut trees, bread fruit trees
and, of course, the house was to be inherited by his first

male child. This was the tradition in Igbonta and indeed, for the entire Igbo people of West Africa.

***

The elders of Igbonta had gathered again at the village arena - *Ama-Omaku* for their *Uka-Orie* meeting. The first item on the agenda was the conferment of an *ozo*-title on Chief Akukalia. He was also known as the *City Millionaire*.

Many of the elders were going round and about the issue, none was courageous enough to hit the nail on the head.

Amaechi finally spoke up. "*Igbonta kwenu!*" 'Yeah!', they all responded. "*Kwenu!*" "*Yeah!*" "*Kwezuonu!*" "*Yeah!*", they concluded in support. "My people," he began, "we know what the land rejects and what our ancestors would frown at. We know what we could do that would bring a bad omen to our land. We equally know what we could do and reap prosperity - long life, rich harvest; yam, cocoa-yams, the multiplication of male and female children. We are all elders ourselves," raising his tone. "An elder does not stay at home while the expectant she-goat labours and delivers in tethers."

"An *nze* doesn't take back his spit. Neither is a titledman known for being *two-tongued*, two-faced or taking a backhander to deny something he said previously. Or that he no longer believes the tradition handed over to us by our forefathers."

"We are the custodians of our culture and tradition. We have the responsibility for handing it on to our children, intact, - yes, unbroken," raising his voice again by way of emphasis. "I'm telling you today, in this *Ama-*

Omaku, that any decision you take in today's *Uka-Orie* meeting of the elders of Igbonta, that goes against tradition, the tradition of Igbonta, the tradition of the land, I, I," striking his chest, Amaechi, Onyemaechi, a free-born son of this land, I," beating his chest again, "Amaechi, hereby wash my hands of any involvement or support. Be it virtual or tacit."

"May the heavens hear my voice. May the earth hear my voice. *Eke, Orie, Afor,* and *Nkwor*, you are my witnesses. Count me out from any ceremony in this land of Igbonta that will offend the spirits of our ancestors. These are the few things I want to say. "Igbonta *kwenu! - Yeah!, Kwenu! - Yeah!, Kwezuonu! Yea-eah*!!!" For more than five minutes after Amaechi's lengthy speech - though he said it was the 'few things' he wanted to say - the whole arena was as silent as the grave.

The silence was broken by Okuefuna, Mazi Chuma Ekwealo's wife who was rushing to get to the market. Okuefuna was notorious for lateness. The villagers were used to her and so no woman would wait and go with her to the market. When other women would be tidying their wares and packing up their baskets to go home, Okuefuna would be hurrying to market like a hen rushing to gather its young ones after being frightened by a hawk. She was also a late night cook. When other villagers would be going to bed, she would be heard pounding her *foo-foo* in her noisy mortar. By the time she finished preparing the bitter-leaf soup, many of her neighbours would be having the second bout of their sleep. She often heard her nearest neighbour, Ogbuagu, Chidimma's husband, snoring. Even when Okuefuna knew it was too late to begin cooking both *foo-foo* and soup, she almost always chose to prepare bitter-leaf soup which normally took longer. She liked bitter-leaf soup very much, especially when cooked with snails and dried fish from Katsina-Ala. Her husband, Mazi Chuma Ekwealo, enjoyed it too. Although he often complained about Okuefuna's lateness in preparing his meal, he did not mind staying wide awake till midnight provided he had his *foo-foo* with bitter-leaf soup. Ego, their youngest daughter, equally enjoyed *foo-foo* with bitter-leaf soup. But she hated preparing bitter-leaf for soup, not because she was a lazy child who hated doing house chores. It not only took her a long time to squeeze out the bitterness, her tender hands were usually left sore after this task.

The market women were now coming back. The elders were still in the *Ama-Omaku* village Square. They could hear their wives noisily chatting away, gossiping, babbling and giggling - though they were still half a mile away. Some of their gossips could even be heard by very attentive men's ears. "Women and talk," one of the elders broke the silence. "Does it concern you?" another challenged. "Women are created to talk and gossip, men are meant to listen and to act," he concluded. "Was it why you beat up your wife last night because you were created to act?" the first laconically teased. Others laughed; some boisterously, some just sniggered, trying to maintain the decorum proper to an elders' meeting.

"Igbonta *Kwenu*!" - *Yeah! Kwenu! - Yeah! Kwezuonu! - Yeah*!!! Give me your ears," the Chief Elder, Odu Offorma, bellowed, calling the college of elders to order. "We shall get back to the farm where we are invited to cultivate. Let's leave our women alone. For us men, we have to talk less and listen more. As our people say, when a man is weighed down by a huge problem, he heaves a sigh. Mind you, he doesn't talk much. What a man will do is in his mind. So, what I'm saying is that I want you people to react to what Amaechi has laid down at our feet. About conferring an *ozo*-title on some people in this land of Igbonta.

"All protocols observed," Orikagu began. "*Tufia*! Stop! *Ichie* Eziafa challenged. "We have a tradition in this land. Igbonta people have a method of addressing the Council of Elders. What does Orikagu mean by "*All protocols observed*?" "You are right, Ichie Eziafa, our people have a way of doing things," many of them agreed.

Orikagu had recently joined the band wagon of modern Nigerian politicians. He was not very well educated in the modern sense of the word, but he was very clever. He had not completed his secondary school education though. So sly and smart was he however that one could take him for a lecturer in any university. "All protocols observed" was one of the phrases he had picked up from his long association with politicians. It was once rumoured that he would campaign for gubernatorial election during the next round of elections.

His eyes were on nothing less than governorship of Ndoni State. Many alleged that Chief Akukalia was fully behind him. "He promised him millions of *naira* for his campaign and lobbying and military trained hoodlums to contain his political opponents when the time comes," said a village headmaster who didn't want to be quoted.

In different parts of the Igbo nation, nascent politicians, particularly the illiterate ones, had learnt how to impress their people. Their most vulnerable victims were the uneducated women folk and youngsters who left school too early to join in the race of *naira-* and *dollar-mania*. These were confused but still showed great admiration for the politicians who could use very high-sounding but disjointed English sentences and Igbo phrases wedded together. "*All protocols observed! My respectable, distinguished, great and noble people of great nobility, e-e-e-e-m* **tata bu** *e-e-e-m*," they would begin.

To a large extent, Orikagu of Igbonta had learnt this art very well. That's why he forgot even the sacred tradition of the town and started to address the elders of Igbonta, including their *ndi ichie* by saying "All protocols observed!" If he had not been halted, a great abomination would have been committed that day at *Ama-Omaku*, the most sacred village arena of the land of Igbonta. Igbonta language was the only sacred language to be used to address the elders and *ndi ichie* in the sacred village arena.

To allow Orikagu to continue to use a foreign language to address the elders of the town and *ndi ichie* was tantamount to an abomination. The sacrifice of two cows was required to cleanse the land and appease the gods and goddesses of Igbonta for an abomination of such magnitude.

He grudgingly apologised to the elders for using the expression, "*all protocols observed*". He spoke at length. Most of what he said could be described as singing empty praises of Chief Akukalia. This was no surprise to anyone, considering that he was one of Chief Akukalia's sycophants. In their heart of hearts, the elders knew Chief Akukalia did not qualify for the *Ozo* title. His inordinate greed and ambition were the only reason why he wanted the prestigious title. As for everything else he had acquired, Chief Akukalia was prepared to cheat, bribe, maim and even kill in order to acquire the title. He saw it as another addition to his assemblage of material 'possessions'. The elders were fully aware of this. They had a choice to make - either to uphold the truth and values of the land or to betray them by conferring the *Ozo* title on him.

The first choice would uphold their societal values while the second would lead to a loss of those values while endearing those who made it to Chief Akukalia - who knows, they might get a 'piece of cake' out of his overflowing wealth. Sadly enough, only Amaechi and a few others stood up for the truth. Some, especially after Orikagu's empty speech, shamefacedly betrayed the societal values of Igbonta which were the fabric of their town. Others maintained a hypocritical silence that gave the go-ahead.

"Miserable wretches, shameless jelly-hearted bunch of cowards! Emasculated cassava eaters!" Amaechi scolded them in annoyance. "What do you think our ancestors would think of you? What values are you bequeathing to the young generation of Igbonta?" he continued.

Indeed, the elders did not stop to think of the long term consequences of what they did or omitted to do.

Whatever had happened to the good old days? some wondered. In those days, men were men - courageous, fearless and defenders of the course of justice. "Whatever has happened to the courage of my people?" Amaechi asked himself.

Needless to say, the *Ozo* title was conferred on Chief Akukalia in a lavish ceremony conducted in the town square. *Ijere* masquerade, *Egedege* dance and many other masquerades and dancing groups featured. The ceremony was ostentatious, the biggest event in the history of Igbonta.

The debate on the suitability of conferring this not only prestigious, but also morally-demanding title on Chief Akukalia brought a horrendous division among the elders of the town. Indeed, the political stability of the entire town was threatened by it.

The polemic centred on the questionable source of Chief Akukalia's 'stinking' wealth. In Ani-Igbo, true titled men do not meddle with wealth of questionable source or 'eat' money the root of which they do not know about. Chief Akukalia's money belonged to that category of wealth whose origin was a conundrum to the entire people of Igbonta. Even people from the neighbouring towns knew him as *onye-ogwu-ego*, one who acquires money by evil means. But nobody from Igbonta, though they regarded him as such, would dare refer to him as such in the hearing of any one else. He was noted for his power to make any of his opponents disappear whenever he wanted. He knew top men and women in government whose protection he enjoyed. "Shame on a government that covers the tracks of evil men," some elders of the town would always spit out.

Whenever he wanted, Chief Akukalia would come to spend the week-end at his home town with a retinue of military and police escorts, with highly trained military despatch riders from the *'Odum Military Training College'* Kaduna, blazing the trail. The scenario was that of a pompous military despot who has just seized power in his country making his first *'familiarisation tour'*. Deafening sirens piercing the air, horns blaring to their highest crescendo. Noise, commotion, pandemonium and confusion everywhere in the town. The villagers would come out to behold with their own eyes; men and women standing in wonder and mixed admiration, children, most of whom would stand akimbo, with mouths and eyes wide open.

Chief Akukalia was said to have houses in some major cities in the world - Paris, London, Rome and New York, where his first wife and children lived. Nigerians living in the US called his mansion there *'Nigerian New York'*. Economically, he was a heavy-weight. He was also known as a political *bulldozer*. No *coup* took place in Nigeria, it was said, without his endorsement.

His real identity was also a riddle to many people, even to the people of Igbonta. Nobody was sure whether he was an Igbo, a Yoruba, a Hausa or from one of the ethnic minorities in the country. Some said his father was an Hausa, his mother an Igbo and his elder brother a Yoruba. Others put it another way round. But nobody was able to substantiate any of the claims.

As one could see, in addition to the clouded origin of his fortune, the elders of the town had the problem of Chief Akukalia's crisis of identity to contend with. The *Ozo*-title was solely for *nwa-amala*, a free-born citizen of the land. In Igbonta, it's an abomination to confer this honour on a bastard, a slave or an *osu*. Because of the uncertainty surrounding his pedigree, many regarded him as the former or an *osu* - at least, by paternal or maternal inheritance. But no one would dare to call him any of these in the town.

***

For some months Amaechi suffered from chest pains and tuberculosis. No one need suspect the truth - that he had been poisoned. Having a premonition of his imminent death, he sent for Tunde and Adiele, his two sons. He advised them to love one another and be united so that no enemy would find it easy to bring enmity between them. "I am not sure if I will survive this illness. Whatever happens, I am sure you will be able to look after your mother and sisters. I still remember the advice given me by my grandfather before he left to join his ancestors. That was when I was like you. 'Always be truthful. Never covet another's goods. Don't be an *ofeke* either...' The same message I am passing on to you today. I must add: Beware of Chief Akukalia and his friends. Whatever happens, never challenge him. You are still too young for that. Our people say, 'If an immature child begins to ask questions about his father's death, what happened to his father will happen to him!'

They both, though devastated in spirit, accepted the message with equanimity and pretended in the presence of their mother and sisters that nothing serious was amiss. In Igbonta such messages were not given to women lest they should die of anxiety.

A week before the ceremony in which the *Ozo*-title was to be conferred on Chief Akukalia, Amaechi died under what might be described as very mysterious circumstances. Ekemma his widow, Adiele, his elder son, and his four daughters were left to fend for themselves while Tunde travelled to the North where he again struggled unsuccessfully to find a job. He later travelled to Cameroon where he was able to secure a job and save some money. That enabled him to go to Paris to further his education.

***

No sooner had Amaechi died than Chief Akukalia, the *City millionaire*, began to claim as his Tunde's *Ana-obi*, the piece of land near his compound which Amaechi, his father and his great grandfather had been farming from time immemorial. Tunde got his mother's letter informing him that Chief Akukalia had taken his *Ana-obi* and started building on it. Nobody could challenge him, not even Adiele, Tunde's elder brother. After all, he was a common bicycle repairer in the village.

Amaechi had designated the piece of land as an *Ana-obi* for Tunde, his second son.

Since Chief Akukalia had come back from New York, he had had the desire to build a swimming pool in his compound - "a necessary appurtenance to the house for my children," he told a friend. His big obstacle was lack of space. Though he had acres of orchards and flower gardens, with electrified fences going round the whole compound as in an area where a military or civilian dictator lives, neither the orchards nor the flower gardens could be dispensed with for the swimming pool. The only alternative was to acquire the nearest piece of land. And that was the land of the family of Amaechi.

Since he had become the 'City Millionaire', Chief Akukalia had changed a great deal. His ways also changed. His former name was Omengboji; ('one who does when he has'). He changed it to Chief Akukalia in line with his overflowing wealth.

For him and his four wives and eleven children, life had only one purpose; jollification and carnal gratification.

He had nothing to do with religion or God. The only commandment of God he obeyed was 'Increase and multiply, fill the earth'. He went on marrying and begetting children as though he were the one and only person charged with the obligation of filling the earth. Wealthy people in Opia and other neighbouring towns were said to use their wealth to provide social amenities in their respective towns. Not Chief Akukalia. Instead, he used the surplus of his wealth to buy mischief and trouble.

People of Igbonta added a new response to the name *'Akukalia'*. *Akukalia - ewelu ya golu okwu n'uka*! When wealth overflows, the excess is used to purchase trouble.

Many believed he was suffering from megalomania, an obsession with self-exaltation and pomposity. His extraordinary lavishness formed a major topic of discussion in Igbonta. It was also a cause for concern to his *Umunna*, who were often ridiculed by other *Umunna* for having begotten a child who was a wealthy *ofeke*, - an affluent worthless ninny.

Earlier, the name 'Akukalia' was so cherished that young men of Igbonta chose it as their ego-boosting title. It was so popular that there were more than ten persons with the title *'Akukalia I of Igbonta'* in a village of Igbonta. Today the name has become so obnoxious that no one wants to have anything to do with it, let alone be addressed by it. To call a young man from Igbonta by the name is to invite him for a duel.

Chief Akukalia had learnt from an elder, the type one may rightly call an obsequious sycophant, that Amaechi had set the land apart as Tunde's *Ana-obi*. As somebody's *Ana-obi*, it is against the custom of the town to give it out in exchange for money or another piece of land somewhere else. One must build in one's *Ana-obi*. This made it extremely difficult for Chief Akukalia, the town millionaire, even to purchase the land, in spite of his enormous wealth. He must get the land. Something must be done. Something was actually done. And he got the land.

***

'The evil that men do lives after them.' I have forgotten who said it but it is true. Those who go to Church say, *'Vanity of vanities, all is vanity.'* I didn't need to be a Christian myself, before I knew this was also true. Similarly, the Igbo people said: *'One who kills by the sword goes by the sword. He who kills with a gun asks a gun to terminate his own life.'* Had I to be an Igbo myself before I knew this was also true?

The above sayings were epitomised in the life of Chief Akukalia. His sudden death was very mysterious. Extremely ugly, too. It was on a fateful Sunday afternoon. He was at his home town that weekend. He wanted to watch a *Blue* film. It was the latest he had bought from America during his previous trip, barely two weeks ago.

In the whole of Igbonta, only Chief Akukalia had electricity. He connected his house directly from a neighbouring town, five miles away from his house. Because he had some flood lights that illuminated his compound and let any passer-by see his house clearly, he once stated publicly that the people of Igbonta ought to be calling him *Onwa-na-etili Oha I*. The name means 'one who gives light to others.

In addition to the public electric line, he had also a very big Lister generator. He had bought it from a company in Scotland.

That very Sunday NEPA (Nigeria Electric Power Authority) as usual acted in accordance with their *motto*: *'Never Expect Power Always'*. Both their name and *motto* had the same abbreviation: NEPA. And so, there was no power. He had been interrupted the previous day, being Saturday, by the same NEPA. Then he had not bothered to continue as his desire had been reasonably gratified. He had watched what was said to be the most interesting part of the film. At that scene, he had laughed so much that he fell off his sofa. His two bulldogs looked at him and looked at each other and thought he was mad.

Power or no power, Chief Akukalia, the town millionaire, must finish watching the film that day.

His two 'boys' (servants) were out. One of them was his primary school classmate, Okezie. Fate had not favoured him. And so, he had ended up qualifying as Chief Akukalia's gate man. They had a break that Sunday afternoon and went to see their respective families. Chief Akukalia wouldn't allow any of his sons who were with him at home to start the plant, though they were now grown ups. It would be as true to say that they looked more like *agric*-fowls. Some of those Igbo children overseas who knew nothing except how to eat, drink, play and watch television. Spoilt by their parents who thought they were now in a new heaven of civilisation. 'They don't understand *Ipo* (meaning 'Igbo'), they don't need it', one of the parents defended them to their nephew visiting from home. Defence? Or symptomatic of an inferiority complex, as Leopold Sedar Senghor would describe such Renegades.

Well, if what I was told was true, it was the language of the *Been-to's*. No doubt, one day I will be a *Been-to* myself. But I doubt if I would speak like one.

Wealth could make some men foolish if not mad. Not only did Chief Akukalia pour fuel into the oil pot and oil into the fuel tank, he tried to wind the generator, wearing his *Agbada;* called 'One thousand, five hundred' by Igbo people. That was when *naira* was *naira*.

'Doom, doom, ... doom, doom', the giant generator throbbed sonorously. And menacingly too. Before Chief Akukalia could pull out the winder, the hem of his *Agbada* had rolled round it. He was drawn to the plant which trapped his right arm. He just embraced the giant generator like a pregnant leopard caught by a good hunter's giant iron-trap. His right side was brutally smashed. Just imagine what a village woman's wicked mortar does to stubborn cassava which stubbornly refuse to ferment. In great agony, Chief Akukalia screamed and groaned. Before his children knew what was happening, he had lost pints of blood.

They shouted and cried for help. Because they were shouting in *oyibo*, their nearest neighbours and some passers-by who heard them but didn't understand any *oyibo,* thought they were playing. The way *oyibo* children play! Their cry for help was ignored.

It was the youngest child who ran to the house of Mazi Chuma Ekwealo. He said something in *oyibo* which Chuma could not understand. He would have made some sense of what the boy said if he had "not spoken like someone holding a pint of water in his mouth", Mazi

Chuma Ekwealo explained later. Because the boy was crying and beckoning him, he however sensed something must be wrong. He followed him to the house. There, he saw Chief Akukalia held captive by the giant generator, rolling his eyes in agony. With no more strength to cry.

"*Alu eme-eh! Alu eme-eh*! The unheard of has happened in the town-*oh*!", Mazi Chuma Ekwealo cried out and ululated in the tradition of Igbonta.

Within seconds most of the villagers gathered in Chief Akukalia's compound.

All hands were on deck to rescue Chief Akukalia. All efforts were of no avail. The giant plant ignored all the tiny spanners used to loosen its huge nuts and bolts.

There was no mechanic in the whole town except Adiele, Tunde's elder brother who rushed in with some tools. He was a bicycle repairer. But what could bicycle spanners and pliers do to the giant nuts and bolts of the giant generator?

At last, a saviour came. Remmy, Adiele's friend, was a motor mechanic from Opia, a neighbouring town. With 11-12, 20-22, 24-26 spanners, heavy duty pliers, a chisel and two big hydraulic jacks, they were able to rescue what remained of Chief Akukalia. He was rushed to the University of Nigeria Teaching Hospital (UNTH), Enugu. His friend and a fellow member of *'Big Men's International Social Club of Nigeria'*, from Opia, Chief Odejimjim flew to Lagos that night to arrange to fly him to London.

Sunday went and the day broke. It was Monday. The British Consulate in Lagos continued to demand one paper or another. Earlier they issued a *refusal of entry clearance* stating that they were not satisfied that the said patient had the intention to receive medical treatment in the UK or would meet the cost of the treatment without taking employment or having recourse to public funds, or that he would leave the UK after his treatment. They seemed oblivious of Chief Akukalia's wealth or the fact that he had a big mansion in Waterloo, London.

The whole day passed. No success.

Night fell. Day broke. It was Tuesday.

Another doctor's report from the UNTH could not be faxed to Lagos. Not only was the Enugu-Lagos line dead, but Nigeria Telecommunications Limited, NITEL Head Quarters in Lagos had been destroyed by fire the previous night. Some said it was the wicked deed of some NITEL and government officials who wanted to destroy any evidence that could prove they had defrauded the nation of millions.

"How can a nation that destroys itself in this way survive?" one old Yoruba woman, Madam Bamidele, lamented. They said she was one of the few women in Yoruba land who had actively fought for Nigeria's Independence in the early fifties.

Chief Odejimjim rushed to Chief Ayo Jegede's office. He wanted to use his radio message system to contact Enugu. They were old time friends. They continued their friendship even after the Nigerian-Biafran war. Chief Ayo Jegede was also a member of the *Big Men's International Social Club of Nigeria.*

"*Yes, are you hearing me*?" he bellowed from the Lagos end. "*Louder, louder, ... yes I am hearing you now, who is speaking*?", the man in Enugu responded. Time was running faster than usual. Yet, nothing was working as expected. And it was getting too late. Indeed, it was now too late for Chief Akukalia. He had lost a great quantity of blood. He had also lost a great deal of strength. Semi-consciously, he muttered a few words. The people near him could only hear him lament in pain: 'Oh my God, oh my God.' For many years it was the first time he had been heard to call on the name of God. His state was hopeless. He looked like a person who has surely crossed the Rubicon.

It was now two months before the gubernatorial campaign and elections. Orikagu was among the first to get the news. He felt betrayed, devastated and disappointed. But who betrayed him? God or Chief Akukalia? Chief Odejimjim saw no point in asking them to send the third doctor's report demanded by the British Embassy. Chief Akukalia had given up the ghost. He died in the early hours of that same Tuesday.

CHAPTER SEVEN

Université Catholique Internationale de Paris or *Marielabonne* Catholic University of Paris, as very pious French Catholic women of the last century insisted on calling it, was the oldest university in France. It was a Catholic University situated in the heart of Paris. Here Tunde met once again the patriotic Nigerian called Nigerianus, his one time class mate in secondary school.

Life could at times be convergence, divergence and re-convergence. The world is now so small. They remembered their old secondary school days. Tunde reminded Nigerianus of his ridiculous wedding hymn. Nigerianus inquired about Funmilayo. "Oh, she is fine. She has completed her course at the UNN (University of Nigeria Nsukka)," replied Tunde. Both of them had come to study at the university. The former had taken to medicine, while the latter was working for an M.A. in Political Science, specialising in International Relations.

Funmilayo had chosen Media Studies and Journalism. In the International examination for candidates doing Media Communications and Journalism the world over held in London that year, she had scored the highest marks, beating even the candidates from the US and

Britain who had access to all the modern facilities for studies.

In the one month she stayed in the UK she made a good number of close friends. Coming from a different culture, however, she was embarrassed when friends asked her from time to time, "When are you going back to your country?"

Funmilayo was now employed by the Eastern Nigerian Television Authority (ENTA) and worked as a TV presenter, in charge of the programme *Face-The-Point* which she herself had initiated. Soon after, Face-The-Point became a household phrase. It was to a great extent an intellectual programme, yet both the literate and illiterate, old and young took a great interest in it. The programme dealt with interesting issues of the moment. She had carefully selected the members of the panel for the discussions: articulate University lecturers, eloquent politicians, skilled priests, outspoken lawyers, fearless journalists, intelligent traders and so on.

When the government in power was overthrown, the new government saw Face-The-Point as one of the classified TV programmes to be scrapped and banned. But because it was very popular in the eastern zone, or most probably because the new government didn't want to give the impression of being a deadly enemy of press freedom, it spared it. But not without watering down the quality and essence of the programme.

Crooked men are often very careful and clever. Also they often appear very saintly which gives them apparent trustworthiness. The ENTA Managing Director, Dr. Ken Udoye was instructed by the Minister of Information, Alhaji Baba Alhaji, to keep his eyes on

Funmilayo and the type of persons she selected for the weekly programme. Nobody with anti-government views was to take part in it. This meant all the people mentioned above.

It was not long before the public realized that their cherished programme was anything but *face-the-point*. They knew the programme was now being teleguided by the government. People who took part in it no longer faced the point. They either covered or veiled the point or pushed it aside. Funmilayo tried her best but could not do anything to save the situation. The only option left to her was to resign. Her predicament was made worse when some simple minded people began to accuse her of allowing herself and her programme to be abused by the government and its agents. Others who were more critical could see the writing on the wall. They could also see that she was no longer happy with what had become of Face-The-Point. During the programme it could easily be seen that though her body was there, her spirit was in wonderland.

***

Having concluded his study programme, Tunde could not secure any medical job in Paris akin to his area of studies, or commensurate with his academic qualification. For six months, he remained an applicant, roaming the streets of Paris like a warrigal completely bereft of its senses. It reminded me of the man I saw in Tokyo, similarly benumbed and perambulating in the busy roads of that beautiful city. This wasn't an indication of mental derangement, - a symptom of hopelessness, though, it could well have been.

Equal minds think alike, people often say. This was true of Tunde and Nigerianus. Both had been to the same school in Lagos. They were in the same class too. They weren't intimate friends then, though. Nigerianus was more friendly with Dayo. They were the two who had composed the ridiculous wedding song. But that had been a young boys prank of olden days.

Since the beginning of the civil war, Nigerianus had grown into a mature and responsible young man. Nonetheless, he still believed very much in one Nigeria and was still patriotically mad about Nigeria. This was in spite of his inability to secure a Nigerian government scholarship to finish his studies. It was refused on the grounds that he came from the South which the government called an *'educationally advantaged area'* - whatever that meant. He had however wondered what could be the rationale of a government recklessly throwing away millions on what they called *Nomadic Education* and yet being unable to offer him a one-off grant to finish his studies. *Nomadic Education* was said to be an educational policy whereby cattle rearers were pursued in the forests and bushes to get them to learn the ABC and Arabic numerals. "As though their traditional counting is not enough if they don't want any formal education." He didn't even bother to ask why fishermen in his part of the country who were much more settled and were also educationally disadvantaged were not covered by the same policy.

Tunde, too, found it extremely difficult to fund his studies. Ekemma, his mother, Adiele and two of his sisters, including Ojiugo who was married to Opia, occasionally contributed some money to help him in his studies in Paris. He was well aware that his family were starving at home.

Being a petty farmer - eking out a living from machete and hoe greased by the sweat of her body, there was no way Ekemma could afford two good square meals a day for her family, let alone have something to spare. The condition of Adiele, her son, a village bicycle repairer, was equally hopeless. The same was true of her daughters. This Tunde knew. He could therefore appreciate the magnitude of their sacrifice. In Paris, he managed as best he could. His life as a student there was indeed a *tug-of-war*.

When he could no longer bear it, he rang the Nigerian Embassy in Montserrat, Paris, to inquire about the feasibility of getting a grant from the government to complete his course. The person who answered the phone asked him from which part of the country he came. "What has that to do with my inquiry?" he quickly thought. "Well, I was born, bred and lived in Lagos all my life, before travelling to France," he answered. "Your parents?", the voice asked another question. "Parents! What a silly question again!" Tunde wondered. "*Ee..m*, my father is now dead." "But which part of Nigeria did he come from?" "From the South-East." "Well, I am afraid", the voice began to explain, "people from that area are not eligible for government grants or scholarships." "Why?" Tunde demanded furiously. "They are from an educationally advantaged part of the country," the voice explained and put the receiver down. Tunde took a deep breath. In and out!

Two weeks previously, a friend from Okene who had been at the university with him told him about one Musa Ibrahim, who, without asking for it, got both government and a Commonwealth scholarship to study history at Cambridge University in the UK. It was said he collected the money, spent a few weeks in London and travelled to the States. Without attending a single lecture. A few months later, he was seen working in the Nigerian Embassy in Casablanca, Minnesota, USA. "As what?", Tunde asked. "As what?" repeated his friend. "I don't know!"

As if to add insult to injury, that evening Tunde got a lengthy letter from his younger sister, Ifeoma. Most of its contents weren't pleasant.

'My dear beloved brother,

... On a sad note I must tell you that the economy is still hopeless. We are in a situation where yesterday was better than today. The most annoying thing is that the condition of things in the country is man made. Nigeria has the wealth. I have just finished my youth service in the North. If you see Abuja, the new capital city of Nigeria, it is wonderfully beautiful. A lot of money is pumped into it. But I don't know whether one is right to call it the capital city of Nigeria or the Islamic capital state of the North. Why spend all that money on Abuja while millions of our people are dying of hunger and ill health? This I don't understand. Rome was not built in a day but they want to build Abuja in an hour.

Tunde, don't say I am bothering you, indeed since I came back to the East I have started asking myself if we really belong to this country. These days when I think about travelling I shudder. No roads! Up North, it is a different story. They have roads and they are good. And I can't help asking myself, are we Easterners actually part and parcel of this Nigeria? I need not tell you of the frequent religious riots in which lots and lots of southern Christians are senselessly massacred in the North by Muslims. The BBC and the VOA must be keeping you informed of all this and of our political set up at present in shambles. Southerners are not allowed by the Federal Government to build industries in the South unless they pay millions of naira. They are asked to build in the North where they are given land free. You know what this means. Use your tongue to count your teeth. I will tell you no more ...

Mum sends her love. One more piece of good news, guess! Ojugo gave birth to a beautiful bouncing baby boy (BBBB) last week. They are both doing well and she sends her greetings too.

I give you my love. Be a nice boy!

Your naughty sister,

Ify.

After reading the letter, he was filled with sadness and joy. Ifeoma was very good at letter writing. She had never written to Tunde less than four pages of foolscap. Unlike many girls of her age, she had a great interest in current affairs. Whenever she wrote to Tunde she would send him news about events and happenings in the country and in Igbonta, their home town.

Despite all odds, Tunde and Nigerianus continued to show great love for Nigeria, their country. Nobody who knew them doubted their patriotism.

It was not long before Tunde decided to take a job - any job. He finally secured temporary employment with a French railway corporation, *Le Monde de la Personne Internationale*. Tunde was employed as a refuse disposer, in charge of emptying dustbins at *Le Monde* underground station. It may not be said he was unhappy with this job. Certainly, he was not happy with it either.

The thought of how one could train as a doctor and end up being a refuse collector, at times, pricked his heart. "One shouldn't throw away bad water until clean water is found," he advised himself. "But how could one continue to do work devoid of job-satisfaction? No job satisfaction! Not enough pay either!," he soliloquised. He spoke so loudly one could imagine he was addressing a group of friends.

Since they had parted in Paris, Tunde and Nigerianus had not met again until that fateful evening. Tunde had just finished his evening shift and was going home. Nigerianus had just come to Paris on summer holiday. Looking at him, one could infer he was doing well in the US. He had a prestigious and well-paid job in a firm in America. He was the *Chief Inter-Continental Consultant Personnel*, whatever that meant.

Nigerianus had forgotten most of his ugly experiences in Nigeria after his first degree. That fateful Wednesday, coming out from the Ministry of Education, Scholarship Department, he had breathed heavily in astonishment, weighed down by a heavy load of anger and anxiety. "One Nigeria", he mocked, meanwhile, forgetting his patriotism. "Hoax, hypocrisy, deception", he said to himself, rolling his eyeballs as he soliloquised like someone in the first stage of insanity.

He didn't know whom to blame - the God who created him? The parents who gave him Southern identity by birth? The colonial British who fabricated the disunited nations of one Nigeria? Or the perfidious politicians or the military scallywags whose major government policy was Dichotomy? "*State of Origin, Quota System, Imbalance, Educationally Disadvantaged States.* And then, *'Federal Character'*, whatever and whenever it suited their ulterior motive," he lamented angrily.

He blamed the problem of Nigeria on Southern disunity. 'Yorubas against Igbos, River people against central Igbos even when some of them were Igbos themselves. Igbos against Yorubas etc. etc. etc.

"Southern difficulty is now Northern opportunity. But Northern opportunity is National difficulty. National difficulty equals national retrogression. What have the North to show as their achievements since they hijacked Nigerian leadership?" he queried, concluding his soliloquy.

Some years in America had convinced Nigerianus that Nigeria must have made some pleasant changes. He read speeches of military coup plotters who toppled the previous military government. Naively, he believed they would work wonders. "At least they will bring order, financial discipline and true unity with their programme", he assured himself.

Forgetting his last and destabilising experience in the Ministry of Education in the North, he convinced himself: "Yes, Nigeria is a great country of great hope for all its citizens." Despite the present internal apartheid! "*Yah*, the present military government is trying to redress the situation." After all, for the past thirty five years, an Easterner had been made Nigerian ambassador to the

United States of America. Nigerianus once again became a very stubborn patriot.

After his studies in Paris, like Tunde, he could not find a reasonable job to take. He searched endlessly but could find nothing suitable to his talents let alone his field of studies. Not that there were no vacancies, but ...

Thank goodness, he succeeded in getting a good job in the States. He advised Tunde to leave Paris for California. He firmly believed job opportunities to be plenty there. "And job satisfaction too," Tunde added in his mind.

It did not take long before he finally concluded he would leave for America. He tendered his letter of resignation. Two weeks later, he went to America.

After twelve days in America, Tunde was employed to work in the *Gamalio City Central Hospital,* California. He worked there for some time before he decided it would be more profitable to do *locum* for about six months before getting back to regular employment.

In the US, Tunde met and married an American woman, Pamela. To look at, she was very elegant and gentle. Her beautiful eyes appeared as heavenly as those of the statue of Madonna in Fatima. But Pamela had one major occupation, one might call it obsession: shopping. She spent the greater part of the week, however, planning her travels.

Pamela was also pre-occupied with a horrendous longing for and obsession with summer holidays. She liked visiting Kenya's animal reserves. In fact, she did so twice every year. Most of their income was spent on shopping and travelling. Tunde wouldn't have minded if this was the only problem. Pamela did not want to have children.

Whenever Tunde raised the question of the need to have children, she made hysterical objections, like a woman forced to abort her first child, which she had been expecting with enthusiastic impatience.

Pamela was content with her two pets - *Ponny* (a dog) and *Dorran* (a cat). "With the two of us and Ponny and Dorran in the house, don't you see there's no space for another child?" she explained. As though dog and cat were children. "If because of the cat and the dog," (he never spoke of the pets by their names), "you think there's no room for a child, then they have to give way to create the space," Tunde countered. But this was the last thing Pamela was prepared to do - Ponny and Dorran to leave the house? Never!

"What's a family without a child?," Tunde wondered.

***

After the Nigerian-Biafran war, or the Great War, as they called it, Ekemma decided to stay at their home town. She was tired of living in a township, especially now that she was getting older. If she were to live in a city at all, not in Lagos. It was a very long way from her home town.

Since Tunde's departure for the States, Ekemma had had many sleepless nights, worrying and brooding over her son. Though she had other children beside Tunde, she still thought about him as 'one eye that owes a debt to blindness' as the people of Igbonta said.

"What if something happened to him in that country that they say exists on the other side of the earth?," she asked herself. Ekemma's predicament was aggravated by the thought that she had no grandchild from Tunde. "People say women in that country don't value children. How can Tunde ever get a child of his own when he has married one of them?," she wondered. "*Gini ka nwa*," what's more precious than a child? our people ask." A rhetorical question. She repeated it three times to herself, directing her thought to the American women.

"Tunde, my bosom child, the child I carried for nine full moons in my womb, the loving child I fed with the milk from my two breasts. May our ancestors guard you wherever you are. The wicked spirits will not harm you. Wicked men will have no power to harm you either. The land of Igbonta will see that no evil befalls you," she prayed, as she stared around in the obscurity of the darkness that enveloped her whole being and the room.

Though she had handed Tunde to the ancestors and the gods of the land, by her intercession, a thing forbidden by her Christian faith, Ekemma's trepidation was not mollified. She remained fully awake all through the night until she heard the first cockcrow which heralded the dawn of the new day. Poor woman, perhaps she had a psychic sense of what Tunde was experiencing abroad.

***

Since his childhood, Tunde had been harbouring one singular ambition, to become a prolific author. He had liked poetry very much in secondary school. He also enjoyed reading novels until he began to practise as a medical doctor in California. Though his occupation granted him little or no time, he still wanted to be a poet, a novelist, a playwright and a ... a writer of any type of book.

Worried that time was running out, late one night, he began to write what he considered would be a book.

Before he started to write, he had given it a title and imagined it would be a 'best seller': THE REIGN OF THE PIGS. What a beautiful title!," he assured himself.

Though he spent more than five hours at his reading table, he only succeeded in writing three pages. Most of the time was spent biting the end of his pen, staring at the wall and wondering what to write next. Pamela didn't even offer him any support. "How many medical doctors are novelists? I just can't imagine!" she managed to say.

Yes, he began to write a book, but he didn't go on. And the beginning became the end. Often this is a fact of life. However, one may like to read the little he wrote. It's an adumbration of how marvellous the book would have been. But I didn't know whether to call it a fairy tale or a satire.

As I read it, again and again, it still looked confusing to me. Perhaps somebody else might understand it better if they were not block heads like me. Then they would be able to tell me what they thought of it - a satire, a fairy tale or a long poem. Let me presume his permission to publish the little he managed to write: verbatim; no abridgement, no abrogation, not to talk of mutilation of another writer's piece of work.

THE REIGN OF THE PIGS

By Dr. Tunde Dasukki Amaechi

Gone are the days when all animals lived in fear. It's His Excellency, Mr. Pig, Yoyo II addressing the Animal

Kingdom of Nagode. Yoyo II succeeded his immediate nephew, Mr. Pig, Wari I on the throne as the paramount executive ruler of the Animal Kingdom of Nagode. His reign had not given him any restful moments. Having suppressed one insurrection after another, from different parts of the Kingdom, Yoyo II was now faced with the great task of re-building and expanding his palace, and of course, of expanding his influence beyond the confines of the Animal Kingdom.

Since they had taken the reins of power in Nagode, things had been in torpsy-turvydom - confusion and anarchy everywhere. Backward ever, forward never!

Animals from Bushybao, part of Nagode were the descendants of their great great grandfathers. Their great and renowned ancestor was BushyBoa. With the conquest of their town in the ancient days, they later came to be known as the Bush Babies. Nobody has attempted to discover how and why they have this name.

After the amalgamation of the United Animal Kingdom of Nagode, in the ancient days of their forefathers, the Bush Babies had been in a dilemma as to whether to take the Pigs as their kith and kin. Their respective modes of behaviour and animal skin were considered a barrier put between them by the goddess, Ottiwa. Ottiwa was the chief goddess of the universal Animal Kingdom. The Pigs and Bush Babies often forgot to offer sacrifice to Ottiwa when due. She had to put in some remarkable marks of dissimilarities between the two animal communities. These marks later became stamps of great enmity between them.

At the border with the Bush-Babies was another big animal community. The inhabitants of this community were the Foxes. Foxes looked simple, but they could be mysterious. They looked like domestic dogs at times. At another time, they looked like tigers. When the former was the case, they were generally considered helpful friends. If the latter was the case, they were taken to be fiendish and terrible foes.

The United Animal Kingdom had many potentials - peanuts and other types of nuts filled the land, different edible fruits and leaves which all animals enjoyed. Omnivorous, carnivorous or herbivorous, there was always plenty for any of them. Ottiwa, the goddess, was a benevolent goddess. That's why she over-endowed them with many gifts.

There were also many animal geniuses.

Animals from other kingdoms depended on Nagode for their livelihood and structural progress.

Though Nagode had many animals who were talented in different fields of animal endeavour, most of their domestic national works and inter-animal relations duties were performed by the non-natives.

The Pigs didn't trust the Bush-Babies. Neither did they trust the Foxes who they believed were very foxy. But the Pigs could not do the work. Being in charge of the domestic affairs of all the animals, and the procurators of all the Animal Ration, the Pigs were always tempted to over-feed themselves before considering any form of ration distribution, if and when it suited them to do so.

Kariwa Community of the Ants had consistently complained about the Pigs' laziness and inability to lead Nagode to progress. "The Ants will never gain anything in their political and economic liaison with the Pigs. Again, I don't repose confidence in the Pigs because, like the Pigs

*in the human kingdom, they can easily transform a palace
of gold and silver into an uninhabitable slum," their
community warrior once told them. I didn't know animals
knew about politics and economics, let alone talking about
it. 'Were they humans who talk about politics?" I asked
myself. However, sympathetically, other animals from
other communities listened to the animal leaders of
Karawi Community speaking. But there was nothing they
could do to help them. Had they been able to help their
own Communities?*

*The Ants were actually not happy with the Pigs,
not mainly because of the indolence of the latter or their
naiveté as leaders. Almost ninety per cent of the Nagode
revenue came from Karawi Community and from some
parts of the Communities of Bush-Boa and the Foxes.*

*The Foxes, though inhabiting the central left wing
of Nagode, had their kin scattered in parts of Karawi and
Bush-Boa. Their long domicile there had made them lose
all feeling of relationship with their own true family, the
family of the Foxes. Many that had wandered away even
regarded Foxes as their arch enemies.*

*'Shall we continue to look on while the Pigs send
us all to an untimely death?' The other animals had
started again. 'They were disgruntled elements,' the Pigs
said. The rest of the Animal Kingdom of Nagode had been
ruminating over this singular question: Why do animals
who are mediocre have more opportunity to control the
affairs of all the animals than the other animals who are
more talented? Why shouldn't we adopt a modern and
more civilised form of democracy - a meritocratic system -
like other animals the world-over. Are we human beings,*

why should we embrace the form of democracy practised by humans?'

The majority of the animals believed that Meritocracy, as they called it, would work better in the Animal Kingdom than Democracy or Mediocrity practised in the Human Kingdom. These burning questions had been bothering the rest of the animals, except the Pigs. Come what may, the majority of the animals had resolved to put a final full stop to these problems in their next 'All Animal Conference', coming up during the next burning bush season.

After that, all the animals will ... eeem...eeem ...

At this point Tunde got stuck. He went through the exordium - half pleased, half displeased. He made some corrections. He went through it again and again hoping he would get more inspiration to continue. After a brief reflection, he accepted the apparent truth, that his whole ambition of writing a book, and that the whole exercise he had just begun, had come to the stage of forward never. He capped his pen, haphazardly arranged his table, and off to bed he went.

***

Tunde, though a serious minded person over some issues, could also be nonchalant. He never complained about the questionable relationship between his wife, Pamela and Banda Brown. Pamela and Banda Brown came to know each other six months after their marriage. Since then, they had been close friends. Their meetings had generally been covert, though Tunde was aware of Banda Brown's interest in his wife. He seemed not to have minded and so made no fuss about it. He didn't actually imagine their relationship to be particularly intimate.

From her hotel room in Kenya - on a summer holiday - Pamela wrote two cards to Tunde and Banda Brown respectively.

"Tunde, All is good. Enjoying the place. Expect me in six days time. How are Ponny and Dorran? My regards to all. Bye! - Pamela.

The card to Banda Brown read:

"BB, my darling, Must tell you, it's wonderful here. It is unfortunate your manager couldn't grant you leave for us to spend this time together. Well, I'm coming back in three days' time. See you at Minnesota International Hotel, New Jersey. Time 6.00p.m. Ring before coming. Tel: (454) 668899, Room 401. See you! Bye! Yours Ever! - Pammy.

Owing to some technical problems, Oceania Airways International Office in Chicago sent a fax, announcing the cancellation of their flight that day from Kenya to New Jersey. Passengers were asked to call and collect their flight fares. It was too late for Pamela that day. The flight fare had to be forfeited as she had to make an alternative travel arrangement to America that afternoon. For a woman who clearly loves her lover, there's no *there's no time.* Pamela had to be at the scene before Banda Brown's expected telephone call.

'Man proposes, God disposes,' people often say. Pamela, inadvertently, posted the two cards, putting Banda Brown's card in Tunde's envelope and vice versa. At 6.00p.m that day and at the appointed hour the phone rang: "*Kirim kirim, kirim kirim.*" Pamela picked up the receiver, enthusiastic it was her lover, Banda Brown. But it was Tunde who rang the hotel and got Pamela on the line. When she heard his voice, she jumped, her heart sinking into her stomach.

Not only did they disagree on the issue of having children, Tunde and Pamela were incompatible in many other respects. Their world views about life and living were entirely opposed. There was no doubt in the minds of their friends that their marriage would soon be on the rocks. It would definitely be beyond redemption when it did.

The amount of money spent by Pamela on her two pets - Ponny and Dorran - it's alleged, could sustain a family of four. She fed, catered for and treated them as though they were on the same level as human beings. The previous week, she spent S3,000.00 on Dorran alone. This was a bill for a session of physiotherapy and chemotherapy treatment given to the cat. Veterinary report, or should I say, medical report, showed Dorran was suffering from *psycho-somatic disequilibrium*, a type of human epilepsy, - I'm not quite sure myself.

☐

CHAPTER EIGHT

His full name was Nigerianus Patriot Odili. Some of his friends in the US simply called him *'Patriot'*, others 'Odili Odili'. To many others and in official quarters he was simply known as 'Nigerianus'. He was regarded as a true Nigerian both in name, and in words and action. For the past fifteen years, he had lived in America, making occasional visits to Nigeria. The last time he visited Nigeria had been about six years previously.

Early in the year Nigerianus got a letter from his old father, Mr. Ekuluo Odili. Musalla their kinsman had just arrived in the US with the letter. The one the father posted about six months earlier had not arrived.

For many years now mail from Nigeria did not reach its destination. The old man did not know this. Understandably, he had been wondering why Nigerianus, his beloved son, had been refusing even to acknowledge receipt of his previous letter to him. He was so furious that after giving Musalla the second letter, he added a message which Musalla was to deliver to Nigerianus orally. Ninety nine per cent of which was actually the content of the letter. He concluded "If he does not return soon, and I die, he is responsible for my death."

In America Nigerianus had heard much about Nigeria. He was very angry with the VOA's and the BBC's news about the events taking place there. He was particularly enraged with people like Sole Soyinka and other human rights crusaders. "Why should they join with foreigners to destroy Nigeria? Anybody who hears what they say about Nigeria would think it is now a hell, quite uninhabitable."

Nigerianus was surprised but pleased to see Musalla in New York. "It has been a long time men." "*Na so in be,*" Musalla replied.

When Musalla had rested from the long air journey and taken his supper, Nigerianus began to ask him for details about home. He read his father's letter, one of the letters sent to him.

"What letter was he talking about?" "But he said he wrote a serious letter about six months ago," Musalla answered. "I didn't get the letter."

"You see, Nigeria has changed a lot. It can take a letter from Nigeria about five months to get to Cameroon or Ghana and up to nine months to get to the US. And that is, if it gets through at all. You do not talk about international mail coming to Nigeria. Ninety eight per cent of it is stolen or torn up when it gets to Nigeria. NIPOST is now an utter scandal!"

"What are you saying", Nigerianus queried. "I hope you are not one of those destroying the image of Nigeria like these so-called Human-rights activists?" Musalla looked at him and replied in his excellent broken English.

> "*Well, me no blame you. You people here no sabi the thing we dey happen back home. Nothing dey function well.*
> *No fuel which we dey give for other countries.*

> *Schools no dey function.*
> *Water no dey run.*
> *NEPA dey make magic like twinkle twinkle little*
> *star.*
> *If you see the roads, especially in the East, you go*
> *think say na the place wey America drop the*
> *atomic bomb for Hiroshima."*

Nigerianus listened attentively to Musalla *broadcasting* his home news in his perfect Lagos version of pigeon English. He was not convinced that what he had heard so far was enough for people to go about soiling the image of his beloved country, Nigeria. Unaware of this, Musalla went on.

> *"The thing wey dey annoy man for that country be*
> *say, this people them call Muslin-Hausa-Falami*
> *Oligarchy no sabi rule the country well. They even no wan*
> *commot make others try. They come say 'Born-to-rule' be*
> *Allah's special birthday present to them. But people no*
> *sabi why Allah no give them also the gift for better rule."*

Earlier, he had had a letter from Dr. Kiri Kiri, a friend and a lecturer at the Lagos State University. Among other things, he wrote: 'The military politicians continue to *dribble* the Nigerian citizenry. But the most troubling aspect is that sycophants continue to organise solidarity rallies in support of **General Onono** from all local governments. Workers are not paid, schools, hospitals and employment are in shambles. Roads are not repaired. Taxes are increasing. They spend millions of dollars buying arms while our people are dying of hunger. Just imagine a father whose children are in desperate need of food but he thinks it is wiser to buy guns and military tanks to defend them. Defend them from what? Security is at its worst, and yet "Onono is our saviour", the imbeciles sing as they pay him homage.'

For Dr. Kiri Kiri to write such a letter in such a tone, something must be really amiss. But Nigerianus could not yet fully comprehend the situation. He felt it was either misunderstood or exaggerated.

"'If he does not return soon, and I die, he is responsible for my death.'" This last statement of his father's seriously worried him. Had he received the letter in question, he would have arranged to travel to Nigeria four months earlier. He must get ready to travel to Nigeria, lest he returned to find his father dead.

Nigerianus did not merely want to visit and see his father. He decided to buy him a car. A surprising present. Mr Ekuluo Odili was one of those olden-days Nigerian leaders who did not own even a car. Their salary wasn't enough for that. Men of great probity. Nigerianus' brothers at home were to use the car to drive him about. He sent some money to Dayo who was now in Germany to buy the car there and ship it to Lagos. It was bought for N100,000.00. N60,000.00 was needed for its shipment.

An appointment Nigerianus had in London during this period was a very big worry for him. There was no way he could meet the appointment and still go to Nigeria within the same period. He was only given a month's leave from his work in Brooklyn. As a matter of fact, he had to go to London to explain the issue himself. The Director of *Dodds and Jones* was a very kind and understanding man. He postponed the appointment for another month.

Meanwhile, Nigerianus had planned to go to Lagos via London. After seeing the director, he went immediately to book a seat in the Nigerian Airways' plane due to depart for Lagos the following day. After making the booking, he checked into a hotel.

Odua was the last born of the family of Mr and Mrs Ekuluo Odili, the parents of Nigerianus. He was happy about his brother's message that he was returning to Nigeria. For six years, they had not seen one another. His joy was unimaginable when he got a phone call from America to come to Lagos and meet Nigerianus. Odua had never been to Lagos before. Although an Easterner, he was more familiar with the North than with any other part of Nigeria. He had lived in Kaduna for many years. He boarded the night *Awala-Awala* luxury bus to get to Lagos very early the following day.

It was Tuesday. After settling his hotel bill, Nigerianus telephoned for a taxi cab which took him to Heathrow Airport. Many travellers to Nigeria were at the check-in counter section already.

"These foolish and unpatriotic elements tell us that Nigeria is a hell. Why do all these people still travel to Nigeria? Even all these white hypocrites and exploiters?" he thought and smiled.

****

"*Oga* your luggage is five kilos in excess. You either pay £80.00 or you reduce it." 'Please I only ...', he tried to understand and to explain, but the lady did not give him time. "This is not a question of '*please*'" the check-in lady barked. He was dumbfounded. Number one shock. "Who employed this type of beast for such a refined post?" he soliloquised.

"Yes, can I help you?", the lady beckoned to a Polish man with two very big suitcases.

Nigerianus was in a corner, pretending not to be watching. The Polish man's luggage was nine kilos in excess. The Nigerian lady simply checked it in. The Pole paid nothing and removed nothing. Nigerianus lowered his head. With his handkerchief, he dried the tears rolling down his cheeks. Shock number two! "How can a Black do this to a fellow Black? No, how can a Nigerian do this to a fellow Nigerian?" he asked. But no expert was around to supply him with an answer.

The departure time was 8.30p.m. By 7.30pm all had been checked-in. They were now all in the lounge looking at the bill-board to indicate the gate number to the plane. They waited and waited and waited. It was past nine when the manager of the Nigerian Airways came and announced the flight was cancelled.

Disappointment smeared everybody's face. "If you can't go, why not transfer us to another airline?", many demanded. By now it was 10.35pm. Nigerianus and his co-travellers were still at the Heathrow airport. All the Nigerian Airways' officials had by now disappeared. "So they can't even put us in a hotel?" some voices said in despair.

Nigerianus could not make out whether he was still in a real world. Was he going to Nigeria or going back to America? When he came to his senses, he decided to get back to the hotel he had left some hours previously. "But my big problem now is the hotel bill," his mind told him. Hotels in the vicinity of Heathrow Airport were terribly expensive.

Odua had enthusiastically arrived at Murtala Mohammed International airport, Ikeja to welcome his brother. Before 5.30am he was there. This was in spite of what happened to him the previous day. On his arrival from Kaduna, looking for a hotel for over night accommodation, he was stopped by five policemen on evening 'duty'.

"Yes we come see you live for Kaduna and you be trader for Mami Market as your ID don show, but wey your national ID. Na N2,000.00 or we take you to station.

He thought they were merely harassing him until he found himself at the station.

"Sergeant, this man is a suspect, over to you." Odua explained himself and everything to his new captor. His small bag and pockets were ransacked by one of the policemen in the station. Only N855.00, a shirt and pair of trousers were found to be with him. The money was taken by the policeman. "But I have no other money with me", he pleaded.

"But you come say your brother dey come tomorrow from US. He go give you plenty dollar," the policeman replied. "But I have no money for taxi or to pay for over night accommodation," he again pleaded. *'Officer, make you give am N50.00, make him go'*, the one at the counter *intervened.*

It was now Nigerianus' fourth day in London. All his attempts and numerous phone calls to get back his money from Nigerian Airways were in vain. More painful to him was his inability to get back his luggage. He had been in the hotel for four days without any change of clothes.

On his second day however, when he had actually run out of money, he rang his friend in Alabama who sent him some dollars in travellers cheque. His hope was to use this money to pay for his hotel bill and to book with another airline. But how could he do that? Nigerian Airways Authority at Heathrow had not released their luggage. He tried to contact Lagos by phone but to no avail. *'All trunks are busy, please try later. All trunks are busy, please try later ...'* was all he heard on the line. He made another attempt at 10.00p.m. No success. At 12.00 midnight, he tried again and heard the same message. But he was desperate to get in contact with Lagos. He stayed awake till 1.30a.m and tried again. *'All trunks are busy, please try later. All trunks are busy, please try ...'* In anger, he slammed the receiver down and wondered whether it was ghosts that were using the lines at that particular period of the night for all the trunks to Nigeria to be *busy*.

After spending six days in Lagos without any clue of what was happening to his elder brother, Odua nearly ran amok. Thanks to some peoples' sympathy and generosity, he was able to get accommodation and later traced the address of one of their kinsmen living in Victoria Island. It was this relation who gave him money to go and make a phone call to US.

He was told that Nigerianus had since left for Nigeria via London. "But why hasn't he arrived?", he asked himself, stunned.

It was after a week that Nigerianus eventually got his luggage. He booked Cameroon Airlines which, they said, would be arriving at Lagos the following morning. He decided to join this airline which he had never heard of before for two reasons. He hadn't enough money to pay for the immoderate fares which British Airways and Lufthansa charged people travelling to African countries, at times twice what they charged people going to Australia which was three times the distance. He didn't want this thought to bother him now. Secondly, the Cameroonian plane would be getting to Lagos in the early hours of the following morning. But in actual fact it never did. He was very much afraid of getting to Lagos at night, even though he did not believe all the bad news he heard about Lagos.

Nigerianus had been wondering what had become of his younger brother, Odua, who had travelled all the way from Kaduna to meet him. It was therefore a matter of great joy and a strange coincidence that they found each other at the peak of Odua's desperation. They were happy to see each other once again after over six years. But the intensity of their joy was marred by the ugly events each had undergone during the past six or seven days.

It was now exactly five weeks since Dayo, Nigerianus' long term friend in Germany, had shipped the car to Lagos. The ship was expected to arrive at Apapa Port after ten days. Sadly, the car had not been cleared before Nigerianus' return.

"It takes time. And one has to pass through many government agents; Customs, Police, Immigration, Army etc. and each of them has many branches which one has to pass through", the clearing agent explained to him. He could make nothing out of this explanation. And so, he decided to follow him to the port to see things for himself.

Getting to the Port to see things for himself, Nigerianus not only realized that it was really difficult to claim back what one had legally brought into the country.

From a distance he could also see that the front and rear lights of the vehicle were removed. A close look revealed that the boot of the car was seriously damaged, the bonnet ripped open. On a closer look he saw that the kick-starter, battery, hydraulic-pot and master cylinder, alternator and many other parts of the vehicle had been vandalised.

Inside, there were no speed metre, clock, radio etc. He did not know details of the boot contents, though Dayo told him he had left something like a medium box there for Dayo's parents with a letter for them also. The box, it was later said, contained DM2,000.00. All these were stolen at Apapa Port.

In bewilderment, he paced up and down. Up and down. Up and down!

Now the clearing agent was finalising issues to bring out the 'empty-car'.

"Oga you go pay N130,000.00 total. Everything: clearing, police money, army money, immigration money, customs money, and of course the official government charge. This one go be in receipt. So, the whole be N130,000.00."

Nigerianus had now begun to boil.

"What do you mean? How much did I buy this car for? About N100,000.00 and used N60,000.00 to ship it. How can I pay almost what I paid for the car and its shipment just to claim it back here in Nigeria?

"How can I pay the police, the army, the customs, the immigration and the government under whose custody it was when thieves stole almost everything in the car -

paying them for vandalising the car or allowing others to vandalise it?"

"Shit!"

Different army, police, customs and immigration junior officers with whom Nigerianus pleaded to reduce their 'charge' (corruption bill) referred him to their different *Oga*, Master.

Each *Oga* in turn referred him back to the junior officer.

"*Go and he will settle with you well.*" For more than five hours, he was being tossed about from a junior officer to an *Oga* and back to the junior officer.

At one stage, one junior customs officer said to him: "*You wan make them sack me for this job? You tin say they go listen to you, na 'please' we de chop?*"

It took Nigerianus N97,000.00 to replace all the parts stolen from the car and to put it back in good order. He least expected it would cost him so much. He was in a dilemma what to do. To do away with the vehicle, he had spent much time and money on? To go ahead and have it as a gift to his father, he had to spend much more. To spend further on the car, he had to borrow and borrow.

"Unnecessary expenses!", he thought in frustration.

"Expenses necessitated by corruption. Corruption necessitated by inept and corrupt and visionless leadership."

He had begun to see things differently. He remembered the last TV programme he had watched before travelling abroad. It was Channel 10-0, Enugu, *Religion, Philosophy & Man,* a favourite Sunday programme. Fr. Onoyima was addressing a group of students from the university of Nigeria, Nsukka and Anambra State University of Technology, Enugu campus. Fr. Onoyima was a good and lively preacher. Many people liked to listen to him preach. He was also an admired speaker in the Sunday programme, *Religion, Philosophy and Man*. He was popular among students who usually preferred to call him *Go-Slow*. Nigerianus remembered his last words to the students in that programme: '*Life will teach you!*'

They spent another week in Lagos doing up everything they had to for the car. They found a driver who would take them down to the East.

One problem solved creates another, you might say. The major problem confronting them now on their way to the East was where to get fuel. The fuel gauge was now reading below one quarter and the four hundred mile journey had only just started.

Nigerianus, though he had been a patriotic Nigerian and an ardent Christian when he was in Nigeria, during the many years he had been in America had never remembered God, let alone said a prayer. But today was different. "Please God, let this fuel get us to a filling station where we can find fuel. Please God, do not disappoint me. You see I have suffered more than enough since I came back to this country," he heard himself praying.

It seems his prayer was effective, for behold there was a filling station a few kilometres ahead. But the queue was very long. However, they had no alternative but to join the long line of vehicles. And wait!

In frustration, Nigerianus kept a surprising silence.

"This is Nigeria of today and you have not seen the real *wahala* yet," Odua tried to calm him and to prepare him for more shock.

"Na de thing wey we de see since this people say na dem wey go continue to rule us, whether we like am or not."

Odua and other millions of Nigerians were daily undergoing these hardships. It was not so much that they had got accustomed to the difficulties as that they had been dehumanised by the prevalent situation. People now behaved and responded 'accordingly' as animals who find themselves in their natural habitat. Only those who still stubbornly possessed full humanness and such people as Nigerianus who had been away for some time had the feeling they were passing through hell in the country.

"Oga you tell me make I fill am. It is N600.00 plus N300.00. N900.00 total."

"But your metre reads N600.00," Nigerianus corrected.

"You add half price fuel and pay. Na so i be. You no sabi say fuel dey scarce for the country?," the fuel attendant explained with some air of authority.

"My friend, pay him and carry out this motor. You think we go continue waiting for you here? Na the poor boy spoil Nigeria? If you want talk, go to Abuja and Lagos, na there those who spoil the country dey!," some others, also waiting for fuel, reprimanded him.

What surprised him more was not the *illegal* and *immoral* additional N300.00 he was asked to pay, but how many people not only did not resist such day-light robbery but gave it apparent approval. He thought about what the other motorists told him and began to lay all the blame on the praetorian government with which the country had been cursed.

***

From Lagos to Benin there were about twenty five check points of either police, army, customs or Federal Road Safety Commission. In most of them they were told: *"Wetin dey for your booth?"* or *"Wey your particulars?"* In some of them, they were briefly delayed.

"Who be the owner of that suit?", the police officer asked, pointing at the back of the car. It was at Ijebu-Ode junction. "Me", Nigerianus replied. *"Wey the receipt?"* demanded the policeman. "Receipt? I have used the suit for more than three years in the US", he explained.

"Ah, na receipt you buy am with I dey ask for. Abi US people no dey issue receipt? You wan tell us you live for America ... make you carry your trouble go jali!" He disregarded them as he walked away disappointed.

It was immediately after Benin city they met real police *wahala.*

"I don see all your papers. Them all dey correct, but you no get CMR."

Nigerianus didn't know what CMR was. He had no knowledge of 'settlement' in Nigeria either. There had been nothing like that when he left.

Odua touched him, *"Give him N5.00, make we go."*

"For what?", he demanded. Hearing this, the policeman became highly infuriated. He put the vehicle papers into his pocket. Off he went.

Having waited for about thirty minutes, Nigerianus went to the police constable, Eboh by name, and demanded his vehicle papers. "You either pay us N50,000.00 or we take you to our Headquarters in Benin city", the police constable told him.

After more than four hours they were still at the check point.

It was now about 8.00pm. One of the policemen who could no longer bear what was happening intervened. He asked that they be given their papers for them to go since it was getting too late to pass through Onitsha. Others scolded him, including a soldier who was there with them.

All of a sudden the other three policemen and the soldier asked Eboh to give Nigerianus his vehicle papers.

"Over my dead body, they have to go to the Headquarters", he swore. Nigerianus had earlier insisted he would not get back to Benin. He did not see the point in making a return journey to Benin that night. Moreover, their fuel had gone down and there was no firm hope of getting fuel again on the way to Asaba that night.

The disagreement between the other police officers and Eboh led to fighting. Instead of seeing them fight among themselves, Nigerianus later agreed to go to the Police Headquarters with Eboh and the duty police officer in charge.

"You see his papers were correct. There is nothing to suspect him to be a criminal ... What is the time now?", the District Police Officer asked Eboh. "Quarter to nine, sir," he replied.

"And you delayed them from five to this time. You see how you people spoil the police image in this country. Sergeant, remove his belt, beret and number, and put him in the cell," the DPO bellowed, his voice as loud as his hugeness.

"*H-u-u-m*!", Nigerianus breathed with some pleasurable release impregnated with mental and physical tiredness. "If there are still some people in position of authority in this country like this DPO, there might still be hope for sanity in the country," he assured himself.

It would be a dangerous venture to try to get to Onitsha that night. And that was Nigerianus intention. He was however persuaded that they should not do so by Odua. Leaving Benin that night, they had to sleep inside the car at Umunede.

The two brothers and their companion, the driver, had to 'wake up' early the following morning, though what they had experienced was anything but sleep. They must get to Onitsha in time to beat the traffic jam.

Would this be possible? There was another recurrent problem. Fuel. Before they got to Upper Iweka it was past eleven. The long line of traffic was moving at a speed less than that of a sick snail. It took them two hours to get to ENAMEL along the Onitsha - Owerri 'road', (if it could at all be called a road), a distance of about one kilometre.

The Onitsha - Owerri '*road*' was too bad from Atani road junction to Ngbuka. Vehicles had to go through gullies and wade through 'road' lakes. It was a struggle to keep to the shallow section.

Their driver was a master of Southern Nigerian roads, but this one defied him. In the course of the expected struggle, vehicles coming from the opposite directions blocked the whole place and it became impassable. They were there for three hours. Hungry, tired and sweating.

Thanks to the combined efforts of some soldiers and some members of the Federal Road Safety Commission (FRSC) which opened the 'road' and got the traffic 'moving'; it took them about forty five minutes to accomplish this task. In more than five hours the homecomer and his companions had not covered more than two kilometres.

Another big *wahala* was yet to come. A few yards after Ngbuka a trailer had fallen headlong into a big erosion gully and its tail blocked what remained of that part of the Onitsha - Owerri 'road'. Meanwhile, their car was becoming hypertensive. A few minutes later it developed full hypertension which shortly degenerated into over heating. Smoke or steam was coming out from the bonnet. Odua jumped out immediately, and opened the bonnet. The top-cylinder gasket had completely melted.

"My man, carry out this 'tokumbo' from the road", some irresponsible and unsympathetic co-stranded travellers mocked him. An example of Nigerian *road rage!* Some responsible ones came to his help.

"Why all this suffering, why all this mess?"

"Why?"

"Why does Onitsha which has the biggest market in West Africa have the worst 'roads' in the world?", he asked. But there was no government around to give him an answer to his question. Those around him, ordinary citizens like him, have been asking the same question for donkey's years now. In his mind, he calculated how many millions of dollars Nigeria gave to other countries every month for motor spare parts. The damage done to vehicles and the people by badly neglected roads was great. He lowered his head and wondered how a nation could inflict so much pains and havoc on itself and its citizens.

***

Many villagers and kinsmen and women came and welcomed Nigerianus. News of his return spread immediately throughout the town.

It was exactly 3.00am when five armed robbers came also to 'welcome' him. They took his video camera, wrist watch, shoes etc. Above all, they made away with the car he had bought for his father. Early the following morning, he travelled to Aba and booked accommodation at *Enyi-Ikenga* hotel. He spent only a few days around before he prepared to travel back to US.

Two days before he was scheduled to travel back, he left for Enugu. That was on a Sunday. At Enugu he decided to rush down to Onitsha that afternoon. He had a message for Mrs Efuna from her son in the States.

He hired a taxi. After the Oji River, just a few kilometres before Awka, the capital city of Anambra State, he could not believe what he saw. A luxury bus had had a head on collision with a trailer. Both of them were plunged into a deep valley.

The bus had been returning from Kano, overloaded with human beings, some standing after all the seats including the *attachments* had been occupied. It was said the driver of the bus had tried to avoid a pot hole. Suddenly he swerved thinking he would get back to his side of the road before the trailer got to the spot. It was too late. Crash! Darkness enveloped the whole scene.

The valley was littered with crushed human bodies. Blood flowed like water from the Public Water Board's main distribution pipe that eventually burst open after many years of neglect.

Nigerianus and other travellers spent hours and hours lifting the dead bodies. His clothes were heavily soaked in blood. People volunteered their vehicles, transporting bodies to the St. Charles Borromeo and Iyienu hospitals, the only ones nearby. No ambulance arrived. There was none. That wasn't in the programme of the government. If they could not cater for the living how could they cater for the dying or the already dead?

All the passengers were dead, seventy five of them, except a nine months' old child suckling the breast of her dead mother. Nothing had happened to her, not even a scratch. Initially none of the helper-travellers believed what they were seeing. If it was easy to explain why nothing had happened to the child, how on earth could one explain why the child remained close to the mother, breast-feeding herself? This mysterious phenomenon convinced Nigerianus there must be a superior intelligence controlling the universe, irrespective of the contrary view of atheistic scientists.

It was dusk before all the bodies were removed from the valley. He cleansed himself with water from some of the pot holes, and changed his clothes. They waited about thirty minutes before the traffic began to move. Slowly, slowly, like a handicapped millipede, they moved out of the ugly scene.

A few kilometres before they reached Onitsha, lo and behold there were toll gates. Lines of vehicles were queuing to pay their toll. Nigerianus could not understand the paradox: 'why do people pay to be killed?' The Nigerian government kept on collecting money from people driving through the death traps called 'roads' it set up here and there.

When it came to their turn, he paid the lady collector N20.00 and refused to accept the ticket. "It is better that that woman, scorched by the sun in the afternoon and bitten by mosquitoes in the evening, takes the money than a group of depraved and lazy government officials at Abuja," he told the driver as they headed towards the Zik Roundabout.

As they journeyed, he reflected on how much bad leadership had affected the lives of many Nigerians morally and economically. It had also affected their religious and social life adversely. Nigerians, he remembered, were a good, honest, hospitable and hardworking lot. Bad government and bad management had made the lives of millions of the people unbearable. He believed corrupt government and mismanagement were responsible for the bad image the country had abroad, and regretted that the government that fouled the air was pointing an accusing finger at ordinary Nigerians as denters of the Nigerian image. "Political instability, insecurity, a moribund postal system, constant power failure, *all-trunks-are-busy-please-try-later* telephone system, constant power failure, bad roads, mischievous leadership, hunger in a country of plenty and so on are what dent the image of the country, not ordinary Nigerians. These things are not hidden and the world knows about them." He then expressed gratitude to Nigerians who had been very patient and resilient in the face of great provocation, trials and tribulations, and thanked God that Nigeria had not become another Algeria or Cambodia.

***

It was time to go. Nigerianus boarded the *Okada* airline from Enugu airport to Lagos on a Monday, hoping to reach London the following morning. Cameroon Airline flew from Lagos-Duala-London, only on Mondays. Check-in was at 5.00pm. He arrived at the International airport about 3.00pm.

After checking his passport and ticket, "Where is a letter from the company where you are working in the US?", one Yoruba man, Mike, working with the airline demanded. "Do I need a letter from an American for me to visit my country?", he wanted to know.

"Okay, wait for me," Mike told him. He waited for more than an hour and a quarter and went back to Mike who again told him, "Go and see the manager in the office." By now the manager had left and gone to the check-in gate for the plane was due to depart.

Nigerianus came back to report that the manager was no longer in the office. But Mike insisted he must see him, but since he had no boarding pass, he could not see the manager. At about 8.30pm the plane left, leaving Nigerianus in Lagos - a city no longer familiar to him.

Good Samaritans are not only found in Samaria. One can also find them in Nigeria. It was now 10.30pm. Nigerianus was stranded, not knowing what to do next. A policeman, ASP, Yahana Atakawa, from the North came to his rescue and helped him to find a place to sleep. He even gave him some money for a taxi. But he had to wait for a week for the next flight to London.

Luck met him again when he returned to the airport the following day. Two immigration officers, Rachel Ego and Stan Chukwu whom he met at the airport were very kind to him. After narrating his ordeal to them, they helped him to find accommodation where he stayed for seven days, waiting for the next flight, without paying any money. It was in a Catholic parish in Maryland. The Parish Priest, a Yoruba, was indeed a good Christian.

Nigerianus was at the airport early enough to make double sure his journey back would definitely take place that day. It was the same Mike who checked him in without an iota of remorse.

However, as he was passing through one of the many customs and immigration check-points, an official asked him to give him his passport for examination. He innocently did so. The man disappeared with the passport and didn't surface again. The plane was now about to take off. He was not allowed to board without his passport, even with all the explanations. And so, he again lost not only his flight but also his passport. 'Life will teach you'.

Nigerianus was in Nigeria for five months trying to get a new passport and a visa. When he eventually returned he had lost both his job and his house, though he telephoned and faxed both to his Director and his land lady, Mrs Baker.

"That is your problem with your country. Does he want me to suffer as a result of how they treat each other in their country?" the old white lady soliloquised after their third telephone discussion.

Mrs Baker, a widow with no living relation, was a very wealthy woman. She had inherited all the property of her deceased husband. She spent much of her money buying corn to feed pigeons in the town centre.

Nigerianus had lost everything. His job and his house. In addition to this problem was the mental anguish of how he would pay back all the money he had borrowed from people in Nigeria - for car, for passport, for visa etc. He was now four months late for his appointment in London. Thus, he had also lost a big opportunity for a lucrative contract.

***

Landing at Orlando International Airport, New York, he breathed a sigh of relief. Seeing organization, courtesy, kindness and efficiency at work, he sighed to himself. He took a taxi and went to a friend's house, tired, moody and dispirited. Going to the visitor's bedroom, he managed to remove only his coat. Lying on the bed with his shoes and tie on, he thought about Nigeria; the ineptitude and lack of vision of those who call themselves Nigerian leaders, the agony of the present generation and the hopelessness of the innocent Nigerian children, and wept. "Why should Nigerians suffer in the midst of abundance - one of the few countries over-blessed by God?" he asked.

Experience, they say, is the best teacher. Nigerianus had visited Nigeria and had seen things for himself. He began to appreciate what Sole Soyinka, Chichi Achebe, Gabby Fawhwemini and others, in one way or another were fighting for. He even acknowledged that he owed Soyinka an apology for having spoken ill of him and his patriotic activities. "Is there any government in the country at all?"

"If his government cannot ensure that the fuel we supply to other countries is normally obtainable in Nigeria, if he cannot stop high level corruption of his agents in the sea and air ports, if he cannot repair very busy, but very bad roads, if he cannot ... and he says he is prepared to hand over a *lasting and enduring democracy*, what is he actually talking about?"

"Does he not mean handing over corruption, armed robbery, bad roads, and general social disorder to civilians? What is democracy after all? And who is certain he is honest enough not to hand over power to himself." He began to reason with himself and to be critical, re-activating once again the critical quality of his primary and secondary school days. He recalled once again his experience at the Ministry of Education Scholarship Department. The truth became blindingly clear. He began at last to doubt the honesty of those in leadership who were preaching 'One Nigeria'.

"Now I see, it is all hypocrisy and deception. It has to take two years for the conception of a *'lasting democracy'* and three years for its incubation. What is the nature of such 'enduring democracy'? Local government election this year, state government election next year!"

"Our politicians are fools, dogs!"

"He throws out a bone to them. They fight and kill one another, struggling for the bone. When they have nearly finished eating the bone, he throws out another one. They begin fighting and killing one another again, meanwhile forgetting he is still on top of them, milking and crushing them. It is all a deception. Nothing is working. We continue to discriminate against people on the basis of *state of origin*." Abue, Yaro and others who called to welcome him were listening attentively. "But you are exaggerating the situation, Nigerianus," Abue remarked. "Now tell me what is working well in the country today - Ministry of Works? Of Agriculture? Education? Water?

NIPOST? NITEL? Nigerian Airways? What? Because one must be an *Alhaji* or in some cases a *Chief* or come from a particular place or know a particular person before one qualifies to head any of these. It is all Allah's special birthright present: 'Born-to-rule'. Soon after Nigeria gained its independence from Britain, it was re-colonised by the Muslin-Hausa-Falami Oligarchy. How can a ruling class that has murdered Merit and crowned Mediocrity King successfully lead forward a nation made up of intelligent people of diverse cultures? Where 'Alhaji' or 'Mallam' is considered the highest qualification and a prerequisite for holding positions of grave public responsibility even when the gross incompetence of the holder is glaringly obvious. How can we ever move forward as a nation?"

"What have they to show since they grabbed the reins of power?" he angrily asked. "Unity," Abue jocosely added, trying to lower his temperature. "That must be the type of unity that existed between Jonah and the Whale, the huge sea mammal before he was regurgitated," Nigerianus said, smiling this time.

"No water, no electricity! No telephone! Nothing at all! Even common letters do not get to their addressees. Thieves and robbers everywhere. In the sea and air ports. Right under the government's nose. It is incredible! Terrible!"

Again, he thought about the innocent millions of Nigerian children without future hope. "These political morons with their party democracy have raped this country. They raped it, yes, but it is the military knaves from a section of the Nigerian army that have murdered the nation."

"Giant of Africa, the giant of Africa that cannot even run an Air Line with only one aeroplane!," he jeered. "People also have no freedom to cry owing to the pains they are experiencing. If you talk, you disappear."

The sudden change in Nigerianus surprised not only his closest friends but all who knew him. Radicalism was not in his blood, being radically outspoken, even less.

"But this is not being radical," countered Yaro, his friend. "It is being realistic and making good use of one's education. "Have you forgotten what Chichi Achebe said about education?" "What did he say?" demanded Abue. "'To be educated is, after all, to develop the questioning habit, to be sceptical of easy promises and to use past experience creatively.'"

"When will you visit home again ...?" another friend of Nigerianus wanted to know. "Home again? Not yet!" he angrily interrupted. "Now I understand." He felt guilty. "When honourable people begin to run away from their fatherland, don't ask 'why are they deserting their land'. Just know that the *unhappenable* has happened."

The following day, the 'New York Express' had a headline: *'Man Loses His Job and House For Visiting Nigeria*!'

CHAPTER NINE

Tunde came back that evening very tired. The "*All African International Conference On Arms and Stability In Africa*" hadn't ended on time.

Professor Okai Bongo delivered a paper entitled: "*African Despots, Billionaire Heads of State and the Future of African Nations*".

Reacting to a question asked by an African student of Mechanical Engineering of the *Danquesmen* University of Chicago, he described some African Heads of State or Presidents as "looters not leaders."

"You know about those African Presidents or Heads of State for five years, ten years and even for life? Now let me ask you a question. If you are an electrician, wiring a house, and you discover after two months, four months, or a year that you are not only doing it badly, but also destroying the house, and that some people have been electrocuted owing to your bad handiwork and inefficiency, what will you do if you are at all sensible?

"And some of us that are called Professors, Doctors and many of those we refer to as the learned men and women in society are nothing but intellectual fools. A gang of rogues use guns, kill our brothers and sisters and declare themselves our leaders, Presidents, Heads of States and Governors. We join the old and ignorant men and women in the village to address them as *'Your Excellency'*.

"*Excellent* is the superlative degree of goodness. Good, better, excellent. We call robbers in society 'Your Excellency'. We call thieves 'Honourable'. Including our Professors, medical doctors, lawyers; those people that call themselves 'legal luminaries'. And even some priests and bishops."

At this stage, Nigerianus remembered a case involving a parish priest in Onitsha. The priest banned his parishioners from attending opening ceremonies of new houses built by politicians with money that had obviously been stolen from the public treasury. Some of his parishioners accused him of involving himself in politics. Two clergymen, one Catholic, the other Anglican, who were perhaps friendly with some rich politicians, accused him of contravening the biblical principle: 'thou shalt not judge so that thou shalt not be judged'. It is not always difficult to find a scriptural quotation to defend evil.

"Don't you see, a society where a robber is *'His Excellency'* and a thief *'His Honour'* is a very confused and sick society?"

For the first time many in the audience began to reflect.

The professor was a very powerful speaker, very articulate too. He hailed from Congo Zaire but was a lecturer at the *Domingo* University of Dar-es-Salaam, Tanzania.

For weeks, Professor Okai Bongo made headlines in different international dailies and magazines. Western journalists continued to nose around searching for his whereabouts. They all wanted to interview him.

Some African Presidents and Heads of State were not happy with the controversial, red hot speech made by

Professor Okai Bongo at the "*All African International Conference*" in New York. They considered the entire speech treacherous.

Professor Bongo in his speech wondered where African nations like Nigeria were heading as Nigeria continued to suffer what he called "a haemorrhage of talented brains".

"Nigeria, for instance, with all its mineral resources and man power is supposed to be the leader-nation in Africa. But like a child deformed from birth it cannot stand erect nor walk, even at the age of forty. It even finds it difficult to make a meaningful and coherent speech. Nigeria, the betrayed hope of Africa," he declared.

After the Conference, Professor Okai Bongo became a *persona non grata* in Congo-Zaire. That was during the reign of President Mobungo, whose people called him 'President Terror'. One Anthropology lecturer, a member of the organising committee of the conference, from Kenya, was banished from the country. Tunde and Nigerianus, two Nigerian members of the committee, were summoned to Nigeria 'for questioning' by the government.

The Nigerian military junta was furious. They said that Nigeria had been particularly singled out for international humiliation and insolence. They demanded that Professor Okai Bongo should make '*international apology to the reputable Federal military government of Nigeria in particular and to the entire peaceful and law-abiding citizens of Nigeria in general*'. These were the last words in the official government paper. "The Official Nigerian Government Reaction".

What caused some of these leaders particular distress was his rhetorical question. In the full view of heavy satellite television cameras he asked: "Why do a good number of African leaders rule like baboons, conduct their State duties aimlessly and relate with their Western counterparts like zombies or morons?"

He also talked about the unbridled arms race by different African leaders.

"Billions of dollars are still being spent every year by different African leaders on arms - weapons of death - grossly neglecting the necessary machinery for life; that which would enhance the living condition of their citizens.

"In many African nations today, the hungry have no access to reasonable health-care. The education in many States is in irredeemable shambles. And our so-called leaders continue to advance the stupid argument: military weapons are acquired for the defence of the people. Or, as they put it, 'It's for the defence of our "territorial integrity", singing the song of their foreign directors who want nothing but an expanded market for their arms.

"For some African leaders to go and negotiate on behalf of their respective countries is like sending a fly to a convention of spiders. More correctly, it is like sending a goat to a conference of lions." He said that it was the manner in which different inept leaders conducted the affairs of their respective countries that retarded the African continent. "This is also responsible for the whole black race being characterised as 'children' and men being called 'boys'".

"To be recognised as men, our leaders must aggressively assume the real role of men and conduct the affairs of our countries responsibly. Is that African President or Head of State with millions of dollars in a Swiss bank, a house in London, another in New York, a responsible man or a rogue? A leader or a looter?" "A looter!", the audience shouted in support.

"Let us continue with our former point on arms. Isn't it more dignified," he asked, with a subdued tone, "for men to die immediately from bullets of war (war that's of course remote) than undergo the pains of disease and hunger for a long time and eventually die?" The audience roared 'yes'. Some clapped. As he spoke, a lady from Gokina, Namibia started to cry.

"What is wrong with you?", her friend enquired.

"Are you not touched yourself by what African leaders are doing? Making individual Africans laughing stocks in the international arena. You may say I am being sentimental. Are you not touched yourself?" her friend nodded.

"Look at different brains from Africa wasting abroad", the friend contributed. "See some of our doctors, lawyers and other professionals carrying dustbins in New York, London and Paris. Some are working as *Megads* in Germany," she added.

"Why is it an offence to have ideas in some African States? Why is it a crime to have the virtue of courage? Courage to speak out against evil and corruption among those in leadership?" These ideas went through their minds simultaneously. She looked at her friend. Her friend looked at her. The Conference was still going on.

"Yet, these wise African leaders consider it a patriotic and reasonable act to starve their citizens of food, health-care, education, good running water, roads, etc. so as to buy guns, bombers and jet fighters for their protection. Is it not for the oppression of their people?

Only those who are moral and intellectual imbeciles could draw this type of scale of preference."

The audience yelled and clapped again, in support.

"Those who, by ballot or bullet, become leaders in African nations, ought to realise that what we need as a people, if we are to survive and make any progress, are, among other things, tractors and harvesters. Not jet fighters. And not bombers.

"More importantly also, they ought to realise that partisan democracy or politics is one of the Africa's greatest enemies. It is a political system that is setting our people against each other." In conclusion, he went on to say: "I am glad there are many young men and women from different parts of Africa, and from different walks of life in this hall. Before I conclude, I would like to add one more point. Tomorrow some of you will find yourselves in different positions of leadership. Some state governors. Some, perhaps, heads of State. Will you join the band wagon, or will you be Moses, the leader who said with his mouth, heart and head, 'Let my people go'?"

"Will you have the virtue and vision to lead and say, 'Remove the chains of oppression and the yoke of injustice in this land and let my long oppressed people go free?'"

When he concluded, the audience cheered and applauded for more than ten minutes.

News about the conference spread to the four corners of the earth as swiftly as wild fire that has caught hoarded petrol. The Voice of America (VOA) and the BBC were covering the conference. CNN was transmitting it live. Sooner rather than later, reactions were coming from different African government head quarters.

Some African despots simply dismissed Professor Okai Bongo as 'crazy', 'an agitator' and 'subversive'. One military dictator in West Africa called him 'a disgruntled element' who went about denigrating the African image abroad.

Only in Gabon, Tanzania and a few other African nations were official reactions affirmative. Some others didn't want to get involved in the controversy in any way.

When Professor Okai Bongo remembered the roles he had played, the sufferings he went through in his teenage years for his country to be independent, he cried. He cried for the Congo-Zaire. He cried for Nigeria, 'the betrayed hope of Africa'. He cried for Africa.

He took after his father, Bongo de Bongo who struggled side by side with Kwame Nkruma, Patrice Lumumba, Nnamdi Azikiwe etc. that African nations be liberated from the crushing hands of imperial colonialism. Among his contemporaries his father was popularly known as De Bongo. On several occasions De Bongo was put in prison by the colonisers for his 'subversive' speeches and activities. Twice had Professor Okai Bongo joined his father in prison. Though he was then still a minor. His first offence was that he said to a son of one of the colonial officers "Reapers of another man's crops."

De Bongo, in his crusade to liberate his country became a *graduate* of different prisons in Congo-Zaire. In his days, he was known in the country as 'Prison Graduate'.

Professor Okai Bongo himself altogether *graduated* in four prisons before he finally left Congo-Zaire for Tanzania. Two prison terms he served during foreign colonisation. Two were during the indigenous government of terrorism.

Since he left his country, Professor Okai Bongo had one single pre-occupation. How to liberate different African nations from either one-man dictatorship or hegemonic despotism. The second phase of the struggle for internal independence.

***

Tunde and Nigerianus knew the implication of this particular act of patriotism - obey and respond to the government summons. Their mother wit convinced them that would mean either imprisonment, disappearance or being 'killed by the armed robbers'. That basic instinct in man forced them to disobey.

Two months later, both were declared wanted by the military government. Different charges were brought against them. In both cases conviction entailed the death sentence. But there was no possibility that they would avoid conviction. Indeed, their case had already been decided *in absentia*.

"Treason. Subversion. Felony. False Accusation Against the Honourable Federal Military Government of Nigeria."

For the second time, they were summoned to come back to Nigeria. This time it was to come and answer the charges brought against them. Now their case was very serious, they of course knew they would be found guilty of the above. This time to be carried out with military swiftness.

Since they had joined the *'African Liberation Movement'* based in America, and publicly associated themselves with such people as Professor Okai Bongo, and Sole Soyinka, they had inadvertently declared themselves as enemy number one of the Federal military government of Nigeria. Some other African governments such as that of Mobungo of Zaire and Mai-Moi of Kenya were afraid of the Movement. A dangerous organization!

Their case was not made less risky by the small but very harsh article Nigerianus, on coming back from Nigeria, published in *The Two-Times International*. He wrote as follows:

THE NORTH - SOUTH PALAVER

I have heard and read with indignation that only Northerners are opposed to rotational presidency. What a pity! Since Nigeria's independence, about forty years now, the North has produced all our leaders - except one or two who came and went as 'victims' of circumstances. What have we gained since then? We have gained 'northing' only gross looting of the national treasury, agony, starvation, and progress in economic and political backwardness. I would have hoped that common sense (I don't mean justice or really true democracy) would have influenced them to say: "Let us now try the South to see if we can gain 'southing'.

Indeed, the Muslin-Hausa-Falami ruling class has ruined Nigeria. They cleverly use Islam and the name of Allah to monopolise power. In whose name do they misrule and loot their country and subject their brothers and sisters in both North and South to incredible agony - Allah's or the Devil's?

Shall we believe that people from the North are not ashamed of how Nigeria is today? Are we to believe that they do not sincerely want a change that would restore the people's dignity - having become for a long time now a laughing stock among the nations of the world?

*In addition to Nigeria being today literally an extension of Hell where its citizens daily undergo psycho-somatic painful circumcision, our so-called leaders have made the name 'Nigeria' internationally a big stigma. Many honest Nigerians today feel guilty to say, 'I am a Nigerian,' as though they had committed a heinous crime for which they must always say: **mea maxima culpa**! - Perhaps there may be salvation in trying the **Philosophy of the Alternatives**. Nigeria: Hegemony or Democracy?*

Some people considered the publication as harsh. Some of his friends defended him for being very frank. No seriously minded person speaks or writes from a positionless position.

***

They were certain of one thing. As long as the government was in power, they would never set foot in Nigeria. This thought troubled Nigerianus most. He knew that for a despot, five years of *rule* or ruin was just an introduction to chapter one of his *book* of sovereignty. "At least for about ten years I won't visit Nigeria", he feared. For the first time, it occurred to him he was now in exile. Tunde was equally worried. They were now both in exile, declared "wanted men".

Tunde needed a short nap before going to evening work. Because of the row he and his wife had the previous night, they were still pulling long faces and temporarily not on speaking terms.

Being a good sleeper, Tunde knew somebody must wake him up about 4.p.m. if he was to go to work that evening. There was nobody else in the house, except Pamela. Ponny and Dorran couldn't do the job. It could only be done by human beings. An idea came to his head, perhaps, a childish idea. Tunde wrote a note asking Pamela to wake him up. "Pamela," the note says, "*please wake me up at 4p.m. prompt. Thanks! Tunde.*" Going to the kitchen, he left it in front of his wife. Pamela was arranging the food items she had bought. She had just come back from shopping.

Exactly at 4p.m. Pamela made a similar note. "*Tunde, it's 4p.m. prompt. Please get up. Thanks! - Pamela.*" Taking the note to his bedroom, she left it on the pillow, close to his temple.

Fifteen minutes later, Tunde was still fast asleep. Pamela, still wearing a long face, wasn't ready to call for a *cease fire* for their war of silence. But deep inside her, she felt the humane desire to wake him up lest he be too late for work. Pamela, like all women, even when they do not have children of their own, was naturally motherly, had a tender loving care. Women's hearts can be very soft. She turned on the radio, raised the volume. This awakened Tunde and got him off the bed.

Whatever might have been her shortcomings, Pamela was also very aesthetic. This was the very first thing one noticed on entering their room.

Apart from toys scattered here and there by Ponny and claw marks made on the wooden furniture by Dorran, their house was splendid. In the main parlour were three large sofa cushions covered with thrilling tapestries additionally ornamented with beads of gold, silver and diamond, each emitting different colours of light as the rays from the table lamp in the left corner of the room gracefully fell on them. The table cover had a superb embroidery too.

New visitors to the house often reacted spontaneously when they entered the room - 'Were these for us to sit down'? Pamela was a woman of extreme high taste. She made the choice and bought the furniture, though Tunde issued her with the cheque.

At the right side of the parlour was a large book-shelf. I wonder if one is right to refer to it so. At the centre was a big compartment for a 30inch television set, video machine, trays and trays and trays - I can't remember how many they were - of video and radio cassette tapes. Neither Tunde nor Pamela ever spared time to watch the video or listen to the cassette tapes. Besides these items, other sections of the book-shelf - I don't know what else to call it - were filled with books. There must have been hundreds and hundreds of them. With the exception of the few medical books Tunde used during the course of his studies in Paris, they were all novels.

Pamela was obsessed with buying things. Her life of prodigality abhorred even an iota of frugality. She kept on spending and spending until not a penny was left in their accounts. Most of the cassettes in the house were said to have been bought by her. She also bought almost all the novels. She felt special a attraction towards captivating titles.

Seeing the books, one would never fail to conclude: the owner or owners, if one likes, must be avid readers. But she never opened any of the books again except the look she had at them in the bookshops where they were bought. I happened, from the corner of the house where I was, to see the title of one of the books: "*The Mad Dog and the Aggrieved Pussy Cat*". The illustration at the front-cover page of the book depicted a dog that was really mad and a pussy cat that looked truly aggrieved.

***

Since the event of Pamela and Mr Banda Brown, Pamela had not deemed it necessary to say to Tunde, 'I am sorry'. That would amount to acknowledging her infidelity and swallowing her pride. Pamela was an active member of the *Women's Liberation Movement*, California wing, USA.

In America, women were said to be masters of their husbands, and known to have absolute freedom. 'Even the freedom to be *unfree*, some said. They were all forms of freedom.

Tunde didn't even want to raise the topic. A week after they had started to be cordial again, Pamela and Mr. Banda Brown drove past him on his way back home.

By the time she returned, Tunde was already fast asleep, having lamented for two hours before sleep finally weakened and conquered him. *Ponny* and *Dorran* were also fast asleep.

He was smoking his fourth cigarette that early morning when Pamela got up. Tunde was not a smoker before he married Pamela. He later took to smoking, hoping to get some comfort and solace from it.

Pamela: "You don't look cheerful this morning."

Tunde: "Perhaps."
Pamela: "Is something wrong?"

Tunde: "Perhaps".
Pamela: "Am I the cause?"

Tunde: "Perhaps."
Pamela: "Or are you the cause?"

Tunde: "Perhaps."

Pamela: "Stop annoying me. What do you mean by perhaps, perhaps, perhaps?" And Tunde responded yet again, "Perhaps." □

CHAPTER TEN

A friend in need is a friend indeed'. Nothing is more true than this saying. After the Nigerian-Biafran war Tunde and Funmilayo continued their friendly relationship.

They would have got married two years after the war but for their respective parents and relatives. Mazi Chuma Ekwealo, then the oldest in the *Umunna*, was vehement in his opposition. The deadly effects of the war were still very fresh in the minds of many Igbonta people. Hitherto, they still lamented the backwardness of their town attributing it to the war which claimed all their 'future hopes'.

I don't know if that was true, but they said many of their people were disembowelled during the pogrom in the North. Some were beheaded as they tried to escape from Lagos and Ibadan. How could such a thing ever happen in our One-Nigeria? Many were said to have perished in the Biafran battle fields, especially in the Umuahia-Ikot Ekpene sector.

"How can we marry to our son the daughter of our enemy?" Mazi Chuma Ekwealo had earlier objected.

Funmilayo's parents, though they loved Tunde and would have blessed the marriage, thought Igbonta people would see Funmilayo as an enemy symbol. No parent would like her child to be an object of hatred in her town of marriage.

The parental matrimonial disapproval did not prevent Tunde and Funmilayo from continuing their friendly relations. They continued to write to each other even when circumstances drove Tunde to marry Pamela.

Since his marriage to Pamela, Tunde had known no peace. Funmilayo couldn't tell Tunde not to marry Pamela. Though she wasn't in favour of the marriage, she kept mute lest Tunde construed her disapproval to be 'usual women's jealousy'. This Tunde himself knew.

Whenever Tunde remembered the advice given to him when he mentioned he wanted to marry Pamela, he rained showers of blame on his stupidity. "Tunde", Nigerianus began to reply, "our people say, he who says 'My friend, I would have told you' is not a good friend. But he who says, 'My friend, I did tell you' is a friend indeed. So, I have to tell you my mind, though you may not find it pleasant. My advice to you is this: 'Don't marry *Oyibo*, don't marry London, Lagos, New York or Paris. Marry a wife'."

***

In spite of being declared wanted by the military dictator, Tunde and Nigerianus went about attending and organising international conferences on matters relating to Africa. They even intensified their efforts in the *African Liberation Movement*. Inwardly however, each was greatly troubled.

To remove one of the primary worries in his life, Tunde applied for divorce. "How could I continue to call her my wife? Pamela who doesn't want a child, can't save a penny, and will not be a solace to me at this difficult and trying period in my life?" he asked himself.

It didn't take long before they were granted a divorce.

In the USA divorce was as simple as ABC. It was a matter of an application. They said it was freedom, though many believed it had ruined family life, the fabric of any healthy society.

At least Tunde was now free of one great worry: Pamela. This gave him room to worry about other *worries*. Life is a battle field!

Yes, life is always a bundle of worries. No sooner has man finished with one worry than other worries compete among themselves to take the place of the resolved worry. That is life also. Nothing but a bundle of worries!

Being a constitutive element of life, if not life itself, worry is unavoidable. And worry is the identical twin brother of trouble. They always go together, though trouble always goes in front of worry. Immediately trouble comes, worry follows. The more man tries to avoid trouble which brings worry, the more trouble tries to befriend man. He who does not want trouble only wants trouble to come to him. And he who is very cautious of getting into trouble will have his loin cloth get him into trouble, the Igbos say. These are facts of life which Tunde and Nigerianus knew very well.

They were now in a very grave trouble, the trouble that would not be appeased until it took human heads. *Treasonable felony*!

"He who does not want trouble or fights off trouble only wants trouble to come to him." Tunde and Nigerianus didn't want a troubled nation. They laboured rather for a peaceful, truly united and progressive Nigeria, a Nigeria devoid of injustice, the injustice which causes trouble.

The more a man fights against trouble, the more trouble he immerses himself in until trouble ties him up. Man is afraid of trouble. But trouble is not afraid of man.

Treasonable felony was the gravest of troubles that could befall a citizen of a State. Being gravest, its identical twin brother was also like it: gravest worry. For the first time in their lives, Tunde and Nigerianus realized the violence of truthfulness and the tranquillity of falsehood.

"Empty and dehumanising tranquillity", Tunde murmured. They remembered what Sole Soyinka once wrote: *'The man had died in all who remain silent in the face of tyranny.'* "The struggle continues!"

The Nigerian High Commissions in London and New York had simultaneously and vehemently reacted against the *'subversive'* activities of Tunde and Nigerianus. They were accused of washing 'our dirty linen in public'. "It is a great act of civil obedience and patriotism", both replied, "not to stand aside and watch our nation decay. If washing our dirty linen in public will make it clean and prevent us from having deadly rashes, then we are doing a most patriotic service to the nation."

The last time he went to Nigeria, Nigerianus could not believe it was the country he knew some years back. "How have things so fallen apart?", he wondered. He remembered when he used only about N500.00 to travel to the US or London and would be treated as a VIP in any shop he entered as a Nigerian. But today, the same amount of money could hardly buy a bag of *garri*. Not only that, any place he went abroad and introduced himself as a Nigerian, he was looked upon with suspicion and derision.

Looking at the faces of people working in different government offices, he could only see aggression. People walking along the streets of Lagos, Aba, Onitsha, Kano, etc. especially in the villages, according to him were "not human beings but effigies of misery."

"Why", he wondered, "can't **General Onono,** the Head of State and his political brothers accept the fact that they have ruined this nation, bow out and give others the chance to see if they could salvage anything?"

For a long time now Nigerianus had been wondering how **General Onono** could be happy to live in the Presidential House enjoying the title of Head of State when his government could not even ensure that the common people could obtain a staple food like *garri* - the simplest food on earth to produce. Other governments made sure that their countries were making progress day by day in the field of science and technology. Food was no longer their problem. What baffled him most was the tenacity and contumacy of **General Onono** and "these political and military nincompoops who insist on remaining in the driver's seat of the vehicle they know they are driving to a hellish ravine." He also wondered, "How can a nation that has murdered merit and crowned mediocrity as king survive and make progress? Where *'Alhaji'* or *'Mallam'* is recognised as a first class citizen and given a position of great responsibility even though his incompetence is glaringly obvious!" This was the second time this question had come into his head.

He blamed *hungry* Southern politicians; the intellectual or educated fools from the South who continued to sing the praises of "these visionless leaders". "Well", he said to himself, "they are not politicians, but miserable and hungry harlots who are ready and willing to spread their legs to anybody that might offer them even half a penny."

Since he had come back from Nigeria, tutored by realities of life, Nigerianus had not only become very critical and analytical in his thoughts, he had also become a young man of immense wisdom. He had once addressed a gathering of Nigerians from different parts of the country saying:

"What is happening in Nigeria today tells us what is going to befall our children in future. We are suffering today as a result of the bad foundations laid by some of those who came before us. If our children are not going to go through the same fate, we must start today to build a Nigerian society anchored in justice, equality and true unity. Let all those who are today monopolising and enjoying what belongs to all Nigerians and who therefore do not care to see the splendour and benefit of justice beware of thinking that the situation will always continue to be the same. Even if they may be in control of all the jet fighters and bombers and all the military hardware in the whole of the West African sub-region. No condition is ever permanent!"

***

Soon after, Funmilayo wrote back to Tunde. "Thank you for your lovely letter. I need not be told you truly love me. I love you too. I know you know that. Indeed I would like us to cement our love in marriage. I would not however want you to fall out with your people for marrying me. It might be a source of irritation to you in future which I would not like. What matters for me is your happiness. But as you have shown in your letter, if your people no longer object to our getting married, I hereby accept your proposal without any hesitation." Having wished him well, she concluded the letter with "Your true love - *'Layo.'*"

It was soon after Pamela and Tunde had divorced that Tunde wrote to Funmilayo re-proposing marriage.

Nobody recognises the importance of a good, understanding, caring and encouraging wife more than a very troubled and worried man. And that is what Tunde was, a very troubled and worried man.

Throughout this period of political *wahala* with the military government, Funmilayo continued to be to Tunde a veritable source of strength and hope. She even visited him once in America.

"Don't worry, it will be all right", she consoled him. "When you are in need of money or an alternative place to go and rest, go to my elder sister's. I have discussed that with her."

"Do you mean a place to hide?" Tunde jovially added. Actually, he was greatly disturbed, though he feigned to be unperturbed. That was how Igbonta men confronted difficult situations. They would exhibit so much equanimity of mind that one would think there was no trouble.

Continuing, she told him she was serious. There immediately sprang from his sub-conscious mind Funmilayo's similar words to him before the out-break of the civil war: 'No place to hide!'

***

The true beauty of a woman is in her character. Physical beauty, yes. But compared to the beauty of character, physical beauty is *pseudo*-beauty. Funmilayo had a combination of both.

She accepted Tunde's marriage proposal not because of his wealth. He had, on the contrary, no more money as Pamela had liquidated all his wealth. Great uncertainty hovered around his life. Yet Funmilayo said:

'No trouble, if only your people would agree'. She just wanted to marry the man she was convinced would be a good husband to her. Even for one year.

Some women would marry money. Some would marry power. Some would also marry Satan provided he had the money. *'Di gbakwaa oku'*, let 'husband go to blazes', they said.

It was even said that one Marima from Opia poisoned her former husband, a school principal, who was so good to her so as to marry an army officer. Perhaps, in the next *coup* her present husband would be fortunate enough to be the next Head of State. Or at least a governor of a state. Whichever way, she was sure she would either be the *First Lady* or a *First Lady* among other state *first ladies*.

It was 5.00p.m.

From the side mirror of his car, Nigerianus could see four men in the car behind following them. Two Blacks and two Whites. Hefty and tall. Nigerianus and his companions were coming back from a conference held in Minnesota.

"They are hired assassins", his intuition signalled. Not wanting to get his two passengers panic-stricken, he kept the thought in his mind. But his passengers' sixth senses also told them that something was amiss. The way Nigerianus suddenly accelerated the car was frightening. They looked at each other and kept silent.

Gradually they drove to a halt at the side of the road where some police men on patrol parked their four Range Rovers, allowing their trailers to drive past them. Later, they turned back and took another route.

Tunde and Funmilayo's wedding at the Methodist Church, Madrid, California, was grand. Relatives of both and friends from all walks of life were in attendance. I believe some foes also came. This time, none of Tunde's relations objected to the marriage, not even his mother or Mazi Chuma Ekwealo. Time may be at times a healer of wounds, especially when some healing drugs are applied.

For one thing, his mother was sure that Funmilayo, being an African woman, would not only value a child, but would be desperate to have one, now she was married. She had decided on the name to give to her first grand daughter from Tunde: *Nwamaka*; Child is a blessing.

After their wedding, Tunde became a greatly changed man. Not only did he regain some of the weight he had lost, he added two more kilos. His problems, no matter how heavy, were made lighter. Indeed, Funmilayo brought happiness to his life. She achieved this by sacrificing herself a lot.

One of the things Funmilayo hated was living in America. Though she liked America, with all the good and beautiful things in New York, Chicago, New Jersey, California and so on, she hated living there. She told one of her friends that she couldn't cope with the loneliness of life in the States. She wondered how on earth it was possible for people to live in the same house as neighbours for years without knowing each other. And without saying 'hello!' to one another. As people came back from work, they quietly slipped into their flats and apartments as though they were strict Jewish observers of the injunction: To your tents Oh Israel!

"It is not the load we carry that weighs us down but how we carry it," Funmilayo always advised Tunde.

A good wife is the most precious gift for a man, a blessing. Funmilayo was the best blessing Tunde could ever have. A good wife is to her husband a weight lifter, a burden remover. All this was Funmilayo to Tunde. Tunde loved Funmilayo and took her as his equal too. Only a foolish man does not appreciate the good qualities in his wife and show his appreciation with a reciprocal love and care. And that is all a very good wife wants: Tender loving care!

***

Since they applied for asylum status at the US Internal Affairs Ministry, Tunde and Nigerianus were eventually issued with the UNO's passports. With these they became citizens of the world and could travel to any member country of the UNO, except their own. The USA however remained their country of domicile. Travel outside America was at their own risk.

Yet, they continued to travel outside the States, risking their lives.

They had only one principal pre-occupation: Nigeria, Africa must be snatched away from the crushing hands of the tyrants and set on the path that led to greatness. Nigeria, Africa must be liberated! That was the crusade for the second phase of African liberation. All their energy, all their life was devoted to the pursuit of this primary objective. It was a rewarding exercise. But they were not finding it easy, as they could no longer differentiate a real friend from a *friendly* foe.

The shortest distance to a human target is his friend. And in a society bereft of spiritual values, with only a few hundred dollars, one's best friend could become one's assassin in the twinkling of an eye. That highest form of betrayal that made the great Caesar cry like a baby: *Et tu Brute*! And you Brutus!

***

For six months Nigerianus and Tunde had noticed strange people regularly trailing them. This was after the first incident that forced Nigerianus to change his route. He had pulled in to the side of the road and stopped when he saw some policemen on patrol. This was to allow the strangers following him drive past him.

At one time, Nigerianus had to report to the Police. No serious action was taken to protect them as the matter was not considered life threatening enough. As a precaution, they avoided sleeping in their houses every night. Nigerianus took extra measures. For some time, he stopped going to work by his car. The assassins could not be deceived. They were professionals in the business. And so, they, too, changed their tactics.

Two weeks. Three weeks. One month. Both parties continued to play cat and mouse. It was not long before the game came to an abrupt, if only partial, end. One of the mice finally got trapped in the cat's claw. It was Nigerianus.

The news of Nigerianus' sudden death created a great shock, both at home and abroad. He was found dead in his house at about 9.00p.m. on a Saturday. Four gun shots were fired at his chest. So merciless and inhumanly brutal were the assassins that they had gone on to gag him with chains, stab his lips with a padlock and cut off his tongue. It was a horrifying scene.

Sooner than later an Inquest was set up by the US government. The summary of their findings was that Nigerianus had died of frustration. *"Died of Frustration*!"

Lie! Efforts were made to deny that he had been assassinated. The investigators and doctors connected with the investigation were said to have been bribed with millions of dollars. But there was overwhelming physical evidence that he was murdered. Shot in the chest four times!

Owing to some leakage of the Inquest 'findings', there was a huge public outcry in Nigeria, America, Britain and South Africa. This forced the government to set up an independent inquiry. This later reported that he was strangled to death by unknown persons.

Forensic tests carried out did not at first give any clue as to who the assassins were. They made every effort to destroy any trace that might lead to their discovery.

But trust the American CIA. Two weeks later some men were arrested in connection with the assassination of Nigerianus. Two Nigerians, two Americans, one Brit and a Lebanese. The Nigerian military government was later implicated in the plot to murder him.

Omnia flux. Everything changes, for everything is in a constant state of change. It is only change that does not change. And so, no condition is permanent.

Barely two months after the murder of Nigerianus Patriot Odili, the military government then in power was toppled by yet another military junta.

To win cheap popularity and support, they opened wide all the prison gates and doors, released all the politicians who had embezzled public funds; *people who had been sucking Nigeria to death.* Some armed robbers, murderers and politicians convicted of murdering their political opponents were also freed. Nigerians in exile for whatever reason were granted state pardons and were asked to come back as free persons. Including Tunde!

Airports and sea ports were thrown wide open. Nigerians and any foreigner could export and import anything outside and inside the country.

It was panic and scramble everywhere. All sorts of things were imported into the country. Mostly useless goods. Rejected materials, especially *Tokumbo* cars, television sets and refrigerators from Europe abounded everywhere. Raw gold and some valuable goods were exported outside the country by private individuals and were sold at give away prices in some places in London and Paris.

Like many that went before them, it soon became clear that the military 'boys' had no definite programme for the revival of Nigeria. Like their predecessors, they too had no virtue, vision or expertise, except that of planning and executing coups and of looting what remained of the Nigerian economy. And so, once again, Nigeria continued to go down the road that led to damnation and ruin.

For Tunde the only positive thing about the change of government was that he was now free to go to Nigeria unmolested and see his people once again, especially his mother, Ekemma and Ifeoma, his youngest sister. Free at least for the time being. But this gleam of joy flickered out as he remembered that the friend, with whom he had shared the vision of a great country and continent and struggled to make the vision a reality had died in exile.

Nigerianus had been murdered by his own brothers for whom and for whose posterity he had laboured!

GLOSSARY

Agbada - A full length and bogus men's attire worn mainly by the Yorubas of Nigeria.

Alusi - Village or town shrine of the spirit.

Ana-obi - A piece of land given by a father to a non-first born to build his own house.

Ba woni? - How are you? (Yoruba).

Chi - One's personal guardian angel or spirit. As short for *Chukwu*, it means God.

Chukwu - God.

Da daa - I am fine, thank you! (Yoruba).

Dibia - A doctor, especially one, who is very good in herbal medicine.

Eke, Orie, Afor, Nkwo - The names of the four market days in Igboland.

Foo-foo - Mashed yam, garri or potato.

Garri - A form of flour used in preparing foo-foo.

Iba - Yoruba name for *foo-foo* or *garri*.

Igo Oji - Ritual breaking of kola nut.

Ikè - Buttocks

Iké - Power

Megads - Night watchmen (Hausa)

Naira - The name of Nigerian currency.

Ndeli - Deep night; between 1.00am to 2.30a.m

Ndi-ichie - Ancestors. It could at times mean very old men of great honour.

Ngene - The village spirit of the river.

Nnanyi - Respectful way some wives address their husbands.

Nso - An abomination.

Nwa-amala - A free-born son or daughter.

Nwada - Daughter, especially those married.

Obi - Head family of extended families who now live in their different *Ana-obi*.

Ofeke- A worthless fellow or a fool.

Offo -o - So be it or Amen.

Oga - Master.

Omenala - Tradition or custom of the people.

Onu-ogene - refined metal gong voice (sound)

Onwelu nnukwu ike - he has great buttocks

Osu - One dedicated to an *Alusi* or a spirit god.

Otio! - Yoruba form of exclamation.

Oyibo - A white person. May be used as an adjective also.

Ozo - A moral and prestigious title taken by men of noble character and wealth.

Umuada - Married women from the same kindred or *Umunna*.

Umunna - Kindred; a group of families of common ancestor.

Wa je nwu. - Come and eat (Yoruba)